The Skeleton Wore Diamonds

The Painted Lady Inn Mysteries

By

MK Scott

Dedication

A big shout out to reader Kim Haddox
who helped with the title.

Chapter One

AN OVERSIZED BANNER stretched across Main Street declaring in four-foot letters that *Legacy Welcomes Gen Com*. If the message wasn't clear enough, every store with a message board spelled out a similar message. Some even offered a buy one, get one free entrée if conventioneers showed up in costume.

The town's obvious exuberance about the upcoming event reminded Donna of her banner waiting at the local copy shop. She turned to her new husband of one week who was driving. "Mark, we need to stop at Wallace's Print Shop to get my banner. I need to get it up before everyone starts arriving."

He gave a gravelly harrumph that acknowledged he'd heard, but nothing more.

It didn't take her stellar investigative skills to know her honey was not pleased about something. "What's up? Are you sorry we didn't get to go on our honeymoon yet?"

"Of course. That's not entirely the issue though. I'm not all that excited about all these gamers arriving in town. I realize Legacy needs the business. Still, the strangers always bring in an unknown element."

"They also bring in dollars and credit cards."

"Yeah. The lure of easy pickings also brings the criminal element."

Donna gave a small snort. There was no chance that gangsters and ladies of the evening would be strolling their manicured lanes any time soon, but kids who thought it was funny switched license plates or captured hapless snakes and placed them in mailboxes. As long as she'd known Mark, there had only been seven murders in town, which had been strung out over years as opposed to weeks. If the pretty coastal town was part of a horror novel, people might think the murders ran in cycles, and it was time for one more. Not a thought she wanted to contemplate. She gave a small shudder.

"You have nothing to worry about. I investigated previous Gen Con events," she told him. "No crime waves descended on the cities where they happened, while a great deal of money was dropped at restaurants and bars. These are people who play board games and dress up as their favorite characters. These are harmless nerds who are willing to throw away hundreds of dollars on merchandise. These aren't thugs roaming the streets and breaking windows."

"You're right." Mark heaved a heavy sigh and turned on his blinker before making a left turn. He seamlessly slid into a line of traffic heading for the business section of town. "The traffic is already picking up. The new commissioner has us manning the convention center and parking lots twenty-four seven, which is patently ridiculous since half of that time the center is closed."

It sounded like a rant coming on. "Have you decided on where our honeymoon should be?"

He gave a hoarse laugh. "I know what you just did there. How about Savannah or Charleston?"

Neither were the exotic locales she'd dreamed of, but money and time figured into the equation. As one of the few veteran detectives Legacy boasted, they couldn't afford to lose him, especially with two of the other detectives on medical leave. If that wasn't reason enough, the inn was entering prime tourist season with warm weather and summer break.

"They both sound good. Let me think about it. I could do some investigation. Besides the convention, we can't go anywhere until the elevator is fixed and the easy access to the inn is eliminated."

"I'd think having an officer of the law sleeping by your side would give you some comfort."

"It does." She gave his arm a slight pat. "I also have the amazing canine security system."

"What system? Did I miss out on something?"

Donna cut her eyes toward her husband, trying to decide if he was teasing her or really didn't get it. "Jasper. I'm talking about my dog."

"I figured as much but became confused when you mentioned security. We both know your spoiled puggle would sleep through a break-in, only to wake in time to bark at a leaf."

"Yeah, I was trying to interject some humor. You've been a bit of a wet blanket lately since the new chief took over." Even though it was true, Donna had worked hard not to mention it. Since she had a reputation for her outspokenness, she'd already lasted three days longer than she thought she would.

"Took you long enough to say something. I could feel you vibrating, trying to hold it in." He directed an amused glance at her as he swung into an open parking space near the print shop.

So much for hiding her feelings. "I was trying to be patient and wait for you to open up, but you never did. What's up with that?"

"No need to talk everything to death."

Mark put the car in park and cut the engine, signaling it was time to get the banner. It also served as the end of the conversation except, she didn't want it to end. If her husband chose not to say anything, it meant that somehow it would be something that would upset her. Her imagination took the bait and spun various scenarios, most of them fairly improbable.

"Donna, I can see those cogs turning. I'm afraid of what nonsense you might come up with. Let's go get your banner, and I'll tell you on the way back home."

"Really?" She had to do a double take because it didn't sound like the man she knew. "Who are you and what have you done with my husband?"

Mark swung his door open and managed a forced laugh before circling the car to open Donna's door. At first, she hadn't been able to see the purpose in it when she could open a door on her own, but it was growing on her. It was a form of respect, and she could get behind that. She waited, not only happy with his gentlemanly display, but even more pleased to see a few of her co-workers strolling nearby to witness it. It may have taken her forever to get a husband, but she had snagged a good one. She stopped in mid-exit, waving her hands to get the co-workers' attention, which would result in them noticing Mark standing at her door. They'd end up mentioning it when they saw her at work next.

Donna darted into the shop, paid for the banner, grabbed it, and practically jogged back to the car in order to continue their conversation. She all but stomped her feet waiting for her better half to open the door. As soon as Mark started the car, she blurted out, "What is it? What's going on?"

"So much for that patience you're working on."

"Come on. You can't tease me, then not tell me."

The engine growled to life. Mark looked over his shoulder as he slowly reversed the car and spoke. "You probably already guessed that no one is happy at the selection of the new commissioner. He's always nitpicking everything, making irrational demands such as us guarding an empty convention center, and then, there are his jokes."

Since he forced the last word out through gritted teeth, she was betting whatever the commissioner said did not amuse. "What did he say?"

"Whenever I comment on an ongoing case, he asks if that is my opinion or did my brilliant amateur sleuth of a wife make it."

At least the new commissioner recognized she was brilliant. Here she was, ready to hate him. Mark, as a thirty-year veteran, would have been the perfect fit for the commissioner job. Since her sweetie professed he didn't want the job, someone else had to take it, but the man should have known better than to refer to her as an amateur. As many cases as she'd closed, she should be considered more of a professional.

"Hey! What ya know? The man actually recognizes my contributions. Here you thought he wouldn't." She couldn't remember Mark's exact comment, but it was something cynical.

They were back in the flow of traffic and heading toward their next stop, the grocery, when Mark made a derisive snort. "When Billings called you brilliant, it wasn't a compliment."

Brilliant was usually a compliment. She cut her eyes toward Mark. "What do you mean?"

He cleared his throat, then reached back to rub his neck, before continuing. "You know those British mystery shows you're so fond of?"

"Yeah. What does that have to do with anything?"

His hand abandoned his neck to hold up one finger as he spoke. "Stay with me. On the show, they use the word, lovely, a lot."

"I noticed that."

"Anyhow, the sleuth might be saying lovely to a cup of tea or it might be used for disgust when she finds out someone trashed her office. It's the same word, but it has opposite meanings. Do you get what I mean?"

Her brows lowered into a V as she contemplated the new commissioner's words. "Oh, I get it all right. What did you say? I hope you told him what he could do with his brilliant."

He gave a slight chuckle. "Figured you'd act like that. It's one of the reasons I didn't mention it. The only reason he does it is to get my goat. I tell him my amazing wife did not help me. I've been doing my job for the last three decades on my own."

Her ire at Billings was sidetracked by his comment. "No help? All on your own?" She used her thumb to point back at herself.

Mark sighed and placed both hands on the steering wheel. "You know what I mean. The man just wants to pick at me because it's been said more than once in his hearing that the officers would have preferred me over him."

"You told me you didn't want the job."

"I don't. If I had wanted the job and Billings still got it, he'd be the winner. As it stands, he's sloppy seconds, and it chafes. Not much I can do about it. It's hard not to react, since that's what he wants, so I try my best not to."

That made for a difficult work situation, especially knowing the populace of Legacy adored her husband. There were more than a few outspoken citizens who wouldn't hesitate to make their opinions known, even going so far as to mention that Detective Taber would have handled things differently. Thank goodness there were no social occasions coming up where she'd have to play nice with Commissioner Numbskull. Even though she'd improved on her polite manner, it wouldn't overpower her desire to spill something on the man, preferably when he was in his dress uniform.

The visit to the discount store for toiletries and other sundries she needed was short. She'd called in her order. All they had to do was wait for an employee to locate the said order and load it into the trunk. This worked well in theory, but there were times when she was convinced she could buzz into the store, pick up what she needed, and be out before the employee arrived with her actual order.

Mark glanced at his watch and pointed to it. "I thought this was supposed to be quick."

She shrugged her shoulders. "It depends."

Her phone chimed and a quick glance at the number confirmed it was Tennyson, her inn employee whom she sometimes referred to affectionately as her foster son. "Hello?"

"One of your guests came early."

"No surprise." The one thing she'd learned about innkeeping was nothing ever went as expected. If something could go wrong, it usually did. "So, what's up?"

"I'd thought I'd put him on the third floor since we got that cleaned already."

"Sounds good. Any other issues?"

"None really. The elevator guys are reworking the shaft. They brought in a jackhammer, and the noise is killing me."

Great! Just what she needed with a guest in the building. In her dreams, she'd mistakenly believed the elevator would be finished and running by the time her guests arrived. On the upside, they wouldn't be working at night when she assumed most of her guests would be sleeping.

"Thanks for calling. You're handling it fine. See you in a little bit." She hung up the phone and turned to Mark. "You won't believe it."

"I heard Tennyson. He must have been yelling."

"He was. It must be the jackhammering. Yesterday they had the elevator box moving up and down. Although it was just a shell." She sighed heavily. "I had hoped it would be finished today. Now it sounds like they're taking it apart, and the guests will be here tomorrow. I'll need to get the banner up as soon as possible. You can help."

Mark nodded his agreement as he maneuvered through the traffic. Donna lifted an eyebrow and replied, "I'll take that as a yes."

"Of course. Just thinking about the elevator. Once it gets working, we don't want guests to be the guinea pigs. I'd rather try it out on my own."

The inn came into view with huge tubs of flowers lining the walk. Her inspired idea of planting flowers in tubs paid off. Tennyson ran the lawnmower over the previous flowers she'd used to edge the walk more than once. It made her wonder if it had been a passive attempt to get out of cutting the grass. The ones he hadn't massacred sometimes became the target of Jasper's urinary efforts.

He gestured to the front lawn as he pulled into the parking lot. "The place looks great.

"It does. It will look even better with the banner stretched across the porch. I picked out some fancy font that should appeal to all those Dungeons and Dragons game players."

"Yep."

His non-committal reply didn't dim her enthusiasm. Once he saw it, he'd change his mind. The car had barely stopped before Donna swung open her door and vaulted out with the banner box under her arm. She'd cleared the porch steps by the time Mark exited the car. Hands around her mouth, she yelled, "Hurry up and get the step ladder."

Might as well look at the banner while she waited. She shook it out to the accompaniment of the jackhammer. It would be heaven if they could finish up by today. The rolled cylinder of vinyl dropped to the porch and unrolled a little, revealing ornate lettering. The fancy black letters stood out on the light blue background but were a little hard to read.

Her hubby ascended the steps to the porch with the stepladder. "Let's get this done."

Mark opened the ladder and took one end of the banner. "I'm glad we left those bungees in place. Seems like we take down one banner when it's time for another."

His resigned tone made her chuckle. "Yeah, yeah." There had been several banners stretched across the picturesque porch. It made the inn more welcoming in her opinion. Not all her neighbors agreed. She'd heard a few loudly compare her use of signage as being no better than a liquor store.

Even thinking about the comment had her grinding her back teeth. As the kinder, gentler innkeeper, she hadn't informed the naysayers that her banners were infinitely classier. She'd sent Ten out to deliver that pronouncement but had her doubts if he actually had.

Once Mark got the first half of the banner hooked up, Donna walked backward, stretching it across the porch. "Can't wait to see this from the walk."

"Me, too." Mark carried the stepladder to where she stood to fasten the other end. The crunch of gravel signaled a car exiting the parking lot, probably one of the construction workers. How they ever expected to get done with all the coming and going they did puzzled her. Her dog walking neighbors strolled slowly past with their standard sized poodle. They stopped to peer at the banner. One even used the flat of his hand to shield his eyes.

Look all you want. Donna grinned at the men, knowing they couldn't find fault with her latest banner.

The taller neighbor waved at her. "Hey, Donna!"

"Yes." She puffed up a little, expecting a compliment.

"Did you change the name of the inn?"

Her expectant expression sagged with the oddness of the question. "Ummm… what do you mean?"

Her neighbor gestured to the banner. Donna cocked her head but had difficulty reading it so close. Mark had moved to the sidewalk to view the banner where Donna joined him. The large banner that she'd chosen with dice and player tokens to represent the gaming theme appeared fine to her.

One of the dog walkers moved closer and gestured toward the porch. "I'm not against changing the name. I think The Painted *Laddy* is more unique. Pushes the envelope some."

Donna narrowed her eyes at the word in question. It did have two Ds! "Sugar! It's too late to have it reprinted."

Her neighbor shrugged and returned to his companion and dog. She could hear their combined laughter as they strolled away.

Mark wrapped an arm around her stiff shoulders. "Don't worry about it, sweetie. People see what they want to see. It took you a while to see the mistake, and you were trying to find it. Maybe you can even make it into a game for your guests."

Just like him to make an accident into something good. "Yeah, I guess I could. Most of the guests will look at the banner briefly. It would be a bigger deal if I were in the business district and everyone was staring at it. If nothing else, it will teach me to look before paying for it."

Instead of answering, Mark squeezed her shoulder and turned his head to dust a kiss across her hair. He could be the sweetest man.

Contentment wrapped around her, chasing away her momentary frustration. She wanted to rest forever in the moment and savor it. Before she even worked herself into the savoring part, Ten's tall figure rounded the left corner of the inn. He waved, then joined them on the sidewalk.

Donna noted the direction her employee came from. It didn't take her excellent sleuthing ability to know Ten had been watching the construction workers as opposed to folding the laundry as she asked. Unaware of her thoughts, Ten put both hands in his pockets and nodded.

"What are you all staring at?"

"Nothing," Donna answered, curious if her employee could pick out the mistake that had her so flustered only minutes ago.

Ten stared in the direction of the banner. "Your early guest came complete with costume."

Mark made a pretend groan, which earned him a poke from his wife. "Oh, boy. See what I have to look forward to?"

"Come on. These are people who play board games. How bad can they be? Was he wearing his costume?"

"Nope. He had this large unicorn mask under his arm. Imagine trying to get that through airport security."

The question wasn't a serious one, but Mark decided to answer anyway. "Nothing wrong with a costume unless it has a great deal of metal on it."

Instead of joining the conversation, she held up her hand. Something was different. She couldn't put her finger on it. "Listen. Do you hear it?"

"What?" Mark dropped his arm and turned around in a slow circle. "I don't hear anything."

"Exactly. The jackhammer stopped." Her eyebrows lifted. "Maybe they're finished."

A long scream sounded from the inside the inn. The three of them looked at each other and broke into a run.

Chapter Two

A BODY WAS splayed at the bottom of the steps. The awkward angle of the arms and legs did not bode well. The rubber unicorn mask had to interfere with his breathing as well. Donna dropped to her knees to remove the mask. "Call an ambulance!"

If he had a neck injury, which she imagined he did, any movement could make it worse. "I need my stitches scissors to cut the mask off. Ten, I think my purse is on the front porch."

The sound of Ten's running footsteps filled the hall as she took the pulse of the man lying on the floor. *Nothing.* No, she refused to accept the evidence under her fingertips. Donna squeezed her eyes shut. *Not another dead body at her inn.* Perhaps unicorn mask person just had low blood pressure, which made it hard to find a pulse. Mark squatted beside her still clutching his phone. "The ambulance is on its way."

"Good." She sucked in her lips as she reached under the mask to use the jugular as a pulse point. Why had the man decided to go downstairs wearing a mask? Everyone knows it's hard to see with a mask on. Why did the fool decide to try the stairs wearing one? If only the elevator company had finished on time, as promised, she wouldn't be bending over her newest guest. Her masked guest could have safely used the elevator.

The cool skin under her fingertips yielded no pulse, thready or otherwise. "We need to start CPR, now!"

"Got it." Her husband placed his hands on the guest's chest before Donna could volunteer to do it. She picked up his wrist to see if she could detect a pulse as Mark labored. Still nothing. She turned his hand over to check out the nailbeds. They were turning blue.

An ambulance siren sounded in the distance at the same time Ten burst back into the house.

"I have your purse! Couldn't find it at first. It was behind a planter."

"Let's cut the mask off." She put the tip of her snub nose scissors under the mask and began to cut. The thick rubber made it slow going with the metal handles pressing into her fingers. Even though her practical side insisted her guest was beyond help, she still had to try. Other people had been brought back by medical personnel that refused to give up on them.

The wail of a siren signaled the arrival of the ambulance. Donna hesitated in mid-cut wondering how many times an ambulance had pulled up to the inn. Sure, people died every day, but she'd prefer if they didn't do it at her inn.

She could hear the rattle of the gurney and the paramedics talking to each other.

A final clip of the scissors allowed her to part the mask revealing the face of her recently departed guest. Ginger hair stuck to a pale forehead. Blue eyes were widened in surprise and the lips formed a rigid O as if in the midst of a cry of outrage.

Tennyson peered over her shoulder. "I'm not sure if that's him."

"What?"

For a guest to tumble down the stairs was bad enough. She certainly didn't need another dead stranger at her inn. Ten blinked as Mark stood to let the paramedics in. A female paramedic jogged up, opened her bag, and took vital signs. At the same time, her young employee shook his head.

"I wish I knew. All I can tell you is some guy checked in with a unicorn head tucked under his arm. At the time, I wondered if he flew and tucked the mask in the overhead luggage compartment. He had a knit hat on and wore sunglasses the entire time I talked to him, which was odd, but not as odd as the unicorn head."

The uniformed woman sat back on her heels and managed a dispirited shake of her head. "Dead." She glanced in Donna's direction. "I know you." Her eyes widened in recognition. "You work at the hospital."

"I do, Norton." She read the name tag aloud as she searched her mind for a first name. "Danae."

"Yeah, that's me. Do you know the name of the deceased?"

She glanced up at Tennyson, aware she'd never even asked the name of the guest who had checked in early.

Tennyson shot a hand through his hair. "I, ah, think it was Joseph Carpenter."

Mark stood in the background with the other paramedic. "Check his pockets. The man has to have identification." A quick search yielded nothing. Weird, but no weirder than traipsing down the stairs with a full mask on.

Danae rocked back on her heels and stood up. "What do you want us to do with the body?"

Even though she knew the question wasn't directed at her, she wanted to tell Danae to take the poor guy far away. Mark answered, which was probably for the best.

"For now, we'll have to leave him where he is. I'll call the coroner since I assume the fall was fatal."

"Let's hope he's in town," Donna muttered more to herself than anyone else. At the hospital, a doctor could pronounce someone dead, which was helpful since the hospital was chock full of MDs. Too bad the era of house calls had long since passed.

"I heard he was," the other paramedic volunteered.

"Thank the good Lord." A heavy sigh escaped Donna. She eyed the paramedics, wondering if they'd gossip about someone tumbling down her stairs. Maybe. In their line of work, they'd encountered much more unique ways to end it all, from rolling off roofs while viewing the stars to accidentally electrocuting oneself while trimming trees. She had even heard recently that a local woman's death was due to eating arsenic to whiten her skin like they did centuries ago. A fall wouldn't be out of the ordinary.

Danae packed up her medical bag and angled her head toward the dead man. "You really should go through the legal paperwork to be able to certify someone's death since you're already a nurse. It would make sense considering how many people drop dead in your vicinity."

Please. Did she have to point out the obvious? Sure, she could do the paperwork, but if anyone caught wind of it, they'd nickname the inn something macabre like Hotel Death. No way would she tempt fate like that.

Mark was already on his phone. It was easy to tell by the tone of his voice that he was in official mode. "Bring in the CSI team, too."

Crime Scene Investigation team? "Honey, we don't need to call them in. It was a simple stumble down the stairs." She crossed her fingers to be sure. So far, the time-honored method of keeping bad luck at bay hadn't worked very well. Her husband cut his eyes toward her and gave a short nod of acknowledgment. Her remark didn't have the effect she wanted.

"What? When? He did, huh?" Whoever was on the other end of the phone must not be saying anything Mark wanted to hear. Even the tips of his ears were turning red. If he were a cartoon character the top of his head would lift up and release the steam that had built up.

What she wouldn't give to hear what was being said. He'd tell her the condensed version or obviously the edition where he'd delete anything that might upset her. Right now, she was betting everything would upset her since Mark's blood pressure was spiking. He needed to hang up before he brought on another heart attack. Her top teeth embedded in her bottom lip as she contemplated taking the phone away from him. Finally, he hung up. Donna let loose the breath she was unaware she'd been holding.

"Come, sit down." She steered Mark toward the parlor. "What's wrong?"

His eyes narrowed, and his lips remained in a firm determined line. It took most of her body weight and strength to push him into a wing chair. Even then, he sat rigid, stuck in permanent outrage. A low clicking sound meant he was grinding his molars together, again.

"Mark, stop the grinding. You're destroying your enamel."

He stopped, grimaced, then flopped back, allowing his arms to fall over the sides of the chair.

"I'm too old for this garbage!" He gave an audible exhale. "Too old to start a new career. I'm trapped."

Oh, this was bad. She sat on the ottoman by the chair and reached for his hand and entwined her fingers with his. "What is it?"

"Billings." He practically spat the word as if even the shape of it in his mouth offended.

"What now?"

Mark glared, which Donna forgave, knowing she wasn't the originator of his current mood. Not only was the commissioner clueless about how a town like Legacy worked, but he felt the need to change everything. Never mind that the way they'd conducted police work over the years worked well for their burg.

"Might as well tell me since I won't leave it be."

"Don't I know it." He pushed himself into an upright position, then flopped back again. "I'm not even sure I want to be on the force with Billings as commissioner. It makes me wonder what type of dirt he has on the mayor to be appointed."

Well, at least that gave a kernel as to what had her hubby so hot under the collar. "Were you talking to the commissioner?"

"No. Clarice, the dispatcher. I'll have to call her back and apologize for yelling."

"I'm sure she'd appreciate it if you did." Clarice never got ruffled despite dealing with multiple phone lines and calling out codes to the street units. Being the mother of triplet sons, who were now grown, probably made everything else look easy.

Mark already had his phone out and was staring at the screen, possibly contemplating calling Clarice. Donna snatched his phone away before he could tap out a number.

"Don't call her now. You're still upset. Give it time. Tell me what had you turning fire engine red."

"I did not turn red."

Tennyson stuck his head into the room to comment. "You did."

Mark gave him a glance that had Ten pulling his head back fast. Donna patted her husband's shoulder. "Spit it out as opposed to taking it out on everyone around you."

He crossed and uncrossed his arms, before finally placing his hands on his knees. "I can't get a CSI team out here."

Technically, Legacy didn't truly have a CSI team like some of the big cities. Their team consisted of on-duty officers taking photos, questioning bystanders, and carefully bagging anything that could be evidence. Occasionally, they'd dust for prints. This was one reason Donna's observations were so helpful due to there being so few eyes to observe and catalog.

"I imagine all the officers were busy with the convention."

"Could be. That's not what Clarice said. She told me that Billings had total approval of when and where a CSI unit was deployed. He's micromanaging everything!"

The color flared in Mark's cheeks again, proving contrary to Donna's belief that talking about it would calm him down. It only exacerbated his state. She needed to put the fire out. *What could she do?* She clapped her hands together as an idea so stupendous popped into her head.

"We can be the CSI unit."

A groan greeted her announcement. "Billings isn't going to like this."

One hand found purchase on her hip. It had hardly been a month since the name Jerome Billings came up in conversations, and she was heartily sick of hearing it. "He doesn't have to know. We take some photos, hold onto the mask, do a back trace of Joseph's day. It may come to nothing. He could be an unlucky fellow that made a few stupid choices. We should at least try, especially when your *commissioner* is tying your hands."

"I don't know." He stroked his chin. "It seems wrong."

"Were you told not to take photos?"

"No."

"Investigate?"

"No."

"All right, then. You might as well take it easy while I find a sheet to cover our guest."

Donna pivoted to leave and was surprised *not* to hear Mark say that a sheet could compromise evidence, like he would normally. The poor dear was past frazzled, having to deal with an outsider who was determined to dominate by not only changing everything but by apparently criticizing Legacy's finest. Part of the appeal of working for the Legacy Police Department was the lack of stress. It certainly wasn't the pay.

She couldn't count on the coroner being prompt, so a sheet would have to serve in case she had any unexpected visitors. As Donna skirted the corpse at the foot of the stairs, she decided it might be time to break into CSI mode before the coroner showed up. She'd take a few quick shots with her phone, bag the unicorn mask, and make a trip up to Joseph's room.

The sound of heavy booted footsteps sounded on the front porch, drawing all eyes to the door. Where the police here already? She hadn't heard any sirens. For once, they had the discretion to not come in, lights flashing.

A masculine voice sounded from the exterior. "Um, ma'am. Something has come up while we were redoing the elevator shaft."

No reason for the foreman to see a dead man stretched on the floor. "Okay. Wait on the porch. I'm coming."

She hurried toward the door. What else could happen? Whatever it was, it would be anticlimactic compared to the mysterious unicorn man.

A large man in dusty clothes and a yellow hard hat stood on the veranda, clutching a metal box in one hand. She didn't recognize it and had no clue how it figured into the creation of an elevator shaft. Donna let herself out onto the porch and gave herself a tiny moment to resume what she assumed would be viewed as her normal non-smiling face. Her forthright sister-in-law informed her that a forced smile made her look slightly manic.

"What's the scoop?"

"Well, ah, ma'am."

She really hated when people called her ma'am. It made her feel so old. "Spit it out."

"Well, I decided we needed to go in deeper for the shaft foundation. The first shaft had some wobble. It worked, even had a few trials that came off okay." He pointed the thumb of his free hand back at himself. "I don't do *okay*. People who need elevators need excellence."

"I agree." At last, something was going right. "What do you need to talk to me about?"

"We found something."

Donna put her hands out for the box, which she was sure he'd give her. No way it belonged to her, but since it was found on her property then it was hers, technically. "I assume you found this box."

He gave a bob of acknowledgment and handed it over. Her fingers curled around the box, but the weight surprised her. "Goodness! Is this made of cast iron?"

"Don't know, ma'am."

There he went with ma'am again. "Will you be finishing up today?"

"Well, that's what I came to talk to you about. We found a skeleton beside the box. Human."

The box tumbled from her nerveless fingers and just missed hitting her toes. When would she ever learn *not* to think what else could go wrong?

Chapter Three

DONNA LIFTED THE coffee carafe and poured the liquid into an insulated thermos she'd carry out to her hard-working public servants. The coroner hovered over the body at the bottom of the inn stairs. Yeah, just another day in paradise, and here she was worried about Gen Con participants getting too rowdy and maybe spilling drinks on her hardwood floors.

The interior door swung open, and Mark peeked in. "Could you put together some sandwiches? I think the boys will be a while."

"Yeah, I can do that. I already called into work and told them there was a family emergency."

His bushy eyebrows went up. "I didn't know you were related to either the corpse or the skeleton."

"I might have stretched the truth the tiniest bit." She shrugged her shoulders and handed Mark the thermos. "Take this. I'll get the nibbles together. Family emergency is always understandable. The other nurses don't hate you too much for not showing up for your shift." Donna paused for a brief second. "So, when is that forensic anthropologist showing up to age our skeleton?"

"Your guess is as good as mine. We're lucky Western Carolina University had a forensic anthropologist. Dr. Kim Haddox has agreed to come and do an analysis on the bones. She's bringing along some students and making it a project of sorts."

"Yay." She did her best not to roll her eyes but wasn't sure if she succeeded. More people and no place to put them. The town was booked solid with Gen Con participants. "I guess we'll have to stack them like cordwood."

"We'll cross that bridge when we come to it. Besides, they could breeze in, do whatever they do, and be gone in a half hour." He left with the pronouncement, leaving the door swinging behind him.

She laughed at Mark's optimism in thinking something would actually work the way it should. Hadn't she expected the elevator to only cost eleven thousand dollars of her hard-earned money? Now, besides money, she had to chuck her peace of mind due to some creepy skeleton secreted under her foundation. It was a base for either a cheap horror movie or urban legend, possibly both.

The paramedics had left a couple of hours ago. The town of Legacy didn't have enough first responders to allow anyone to sit around and wait. The coroner would call in assistance when needed.

The jingle of dog tags heralded Jasper's appearance. For a change, Tennyson trailed the dog. "Anything you need me to do?"

"Keep Jasper out of the way as you have been doing."

With the pudgy puggle following him, the lanky employee retraced his steps and mumbled, "We'll be in my room watching reruns of Lassie."

"Got it." She bustled around the kitchen putting together sandwiches. At least the deceased would be gone before her living guests arrived. With any luck, she could get Mark to work his magic and hush things up. Thank goodness for Gen Con. Legacy only had one newspaper, and it was busy covering everything related to the convention.

When ham and cheese sandwiches were assembled, Donna snagged a bag of local potato chips to round out the snack. People expected to be offered food and at the very least a drink when they entered someone's home south of the Mason Dixon line. It was the right thing to do, even if their visit wasn't due to the best circumstance. A little food and mulling over the details of a case was what had turned Mark into a serial visitor. After an interlude of eating and chatting, the man decided he couldn't live without her. Maybe it hadn't happened exactly like that, but she did know people tended to relax when fed, which led to informational tidbits. Her foray into the parlor would also garner some of those enlightening nuggets.

Detective Wells smiled up at her as she entered the room. Her first encounter with the young detective occurred back when she had some troubles with a high school reunion. Not only was he one not to miss a clue, but he also had excellent manners. "Hello, Detective Wells. Good to have you here."

Her husband lifted an eyebrow. Sure, she knew she sounded like it was her doing. It was her inn so it followed that whatever went on under the roof, she was the contact person. Too bad the sarcastic commissioner, who had already informed Mark that he didn't want his wife involved, didn't understand this basic fact. How could she not be involved when everything was happening at her inn?

Wells lifted a hand in response. "Nice to see you, too. Sorry about the circumstances."

"Me, too. Find out anything interesting?"

Mark waggled both eyebrows letting her know what he thought of her curiosity. The new chief could be difficult, but he needed to get over himself. Without her help, some of those murder cases would have taken much longer to solve or may not have been solved at all. Unlike anyone else on this case, with possibly the exception of her husband, she had a personal investment, which meant she had much more at stake.

The coroner sauntered into the room, spotted the food, and

whistled. "Done! I was hoping for coffee. Looks like I hit the jackpot!"

Before the middle-aged man could grab a sandwich, Donna inserted her body in front of the platter. "Have you washed your hands?"

His right hand flattened against his chest. "Really? You're asking me that. I should have expected as much, you being a nurse and all. Of course, I washed my hands. Twice even."

If she were handling a dead body, she'd have washed her hands a half dozen times before chowing down. "Okay, then." Donna moved out of the way. "I'll get some plates."

The coroner already had picked up a sandwich and made headway, while dribbling crumbs onto the carpet. He hesitated in his chewing long enough to say, "Don't bother."

Before she could reply to the man who was leaving an open invitation to bugs to come marching into her house, Mark leaned forward and spoke to the coroner in a sotto whisper. "Humor her."

Yeah, as much as she hated to admit it, a few words from her husband would do the job. A woman could talk all day, but a few words from another man often had the same effect as the heavens parting and a sacred text descending from on high. She hurried into the kitchen to grab the plates and rushed back just in time to hear the coroner.

"Yeah, I called my guys to pick up the body. They'll take him to the city morgue. We were able to call up a fingerprint record for Joseph Carpenter from when he was fingerprinted for Child Find. He's older now, but fingerprints never change. It's him."

Donna stood in the hallway, eavesdropping. They had identified the man, which meant she had no mysterious corpse in her hallway, but it left so many other questions unanswered. Why did he come so early? What was with the unicorn mask? The one question she didn't want to ask, since it would open a can of worms, crouched at the corner of her mind. What if it hadn't been a simple stumble?

Wells' voice joined the conversation. "Good thing we had that portable fingerprint identification unit on hand. Anything else we should know?"

The coroner cleared his throat, making Donna debate if she should continue listening in the hallway or enter the room to keep her carpet crumbs free with the plates she held. She took two steps, but then stopped as the coroner spoke.

"Liver was colder than it should be considering the apparent time of death."

Her lips pressed together as the fingers of apprehension grabbed the back of her neck and twisted. Not what she wanted to hear, but not totally unexpected. That is what she thought when she picked up Carpenter's hand and observed his blue nailbeds, which didn't usually occur until at least thirty minutes after death.

Enough. She could only listen to so much without remarking. She strode into the room and passed out the plates. In her rushing around, not only did she not get upstairs to check Joseph's room, she also hadn't checked on the elevator crew. "Mark, did you ask—"

"They headed out to another work site. Told me to give them a call when the shaft was open for work again."

They snuck out without saying a word to her, the person who actually hired them. "Fiddlesticks!" She gave a light stomp with one foot, which made Mark chuckle.

"It's no wonder they didn't talk to you."

"Come on. You know better. Men tend to talk to men if given half the chance."

Her husband gave her a broad wink. "It's because you women

scare the bejesus out of us."

"Yeah, that's so not true." Donna pulled up one of the folding chairs she brought in for her unexpected guests and moved it closer to the coroner. "I heard what you said about the liver temperature. I noticed the fingernail beds were blue. What do you think?"

The man took another bite of his sandwich which finished it off, then wagged his index finger in her direction. "Oh, I heard about you. Everyone in Legacy has heard about you."

That didn't sound good. "Should I ask what they're saying?"

"You have the tenacity of a snapping turtle, the belligerence of a wolverine, and the memory of an elephant."

Her lips pursed as she considered if any of the descriptions were the least bit flattering. "Well, if you know all that, then you know I don't give up easily. In my opinion the man I found at the bottom of the steps was already dead when he took his swan dive or was there for a while and it wasn't him we heard scream."

"Yeah." The coroner agreed and shot Mark a look. "She's as good as you told me she was." He twisted in his chair to talk to Donna. "I know you did a preliminary examination. I'm sure you noticed he didn't have a broken neck."

"I hadn't gotten that far. What killed him?"

Instead of answering, the man reached for another sandwich. He chomped down on the sandwich, delaying his response. Donna hooked her fingers under the seat of her chair to keep from lunging across the room and knocking the sandwich out of the coroner's hand. How could he lob a verbal grenade like that and start chewing, knowing good and well everyone was waiting for the follow-up?

Mark gave her a nod, then spoke. "So, Oscar, you forgot to tell us what you thought killed the man?"

"Oh yeah, that." He took another bite and chewed. "I'll need to get him on the slab before I give you anything conclusive."

Her eyes rolled upward on their own. Talk about grandstanding. "Please. I know you have an initial assumption. What is it?" Medical professionals usually could deduce from simple factors such as the angle of the body, the color of the skin, or the smell of the breath. Other things such as ligature marks or obvious gunshot or stab wounds told the tale.

"Allergic reaction. His throat and sinuses were swollen. He could have been anaphylactic."

An allergic reaction, which meant it could have been unintentional. Even those who were stringent about checking out the ingredients of whatever they put in their body made mistakes. Unfortunately, even though there were supposed to be warnings on food packages, especially when it came to milk and tree nuts, not all companies complied, especially foreign companies. Too often, they were afraid competitors would take the ingredients list and make a competing product. Most with severe allergies carried epi-pens for just such a case. If he had an undiagnosed latex allergy, even the mask could have been fatal.

"I'd be interested in your final results."

The coroner shook his head. "I have a feeling you'll hear about the results even if I don't personally call you."

Donna suspected as much but settled for a simple shrug, not wanting to get her husband in trouble about giving away information about a case. What she did deduce was Joseph must have already been in anaphylaxis shock when he checked in for the time of death to be right. Maybe Tennyson noticed something. The scream they heard couldn't have been Joseph's. It could have been a nosy worker who had come inside to use the facilities and noticed the body. Not that any of the men would confess to that.

As soon as the parlor cleared, she'd grill Tennyson. He could have noticed something even without being aware. It bothered her that Tennyson mentioned the man arrived with a knit hat and sunglasses on, although it wasn't that unusual for a young person. They all donned those beanie caps thinking it made them look hip. Personally, it reminded her of the cat burglars from the late seventies shows.

It was already full summer in the South, which meant heat and humidity. A straw fedora or even a baseball cap would be understandable to filter out the sun's rays. If the man had thinning hair, he may have used it to hide his baldness. All she could remember was his wet ginger hair stuck to his skin. It made it hard to decide if his hair was thinning or not.

As a natural blonde, she envied redheads because they were supposed to have the most hair. Maybe she needed to take another look just to be sure. It had been a couple of hours, which was plenty of time for the hair to dry out. She stood without comment and headed for the door.

Mark noticed and asked, "Where are you going?"

Without thinking, she replied, "To go look at unicorn man."

Oscar yelled after her, "Why don't you take a picture?"

She knew the man thought he was being funny, but those who worked with dead people usually had a slightly off-kilter sense of humor. Their patients never laughed, so it would be hard for them to measure what was funny and what wasn't. His suggestion had merit and her phone was in her pocket. She would take a picture. Several. What she couldn't do is touch the body. There could already be her initial fingerprints on the man's wrist and neck where she checked his pulse.

Then again, there was no reason for someone to be pulling

prints from someone who had an allergic reaction and stumbled down the stairs. Surely the man would have recognized his own condition. Had he been sweating when he entered the inn? Another question for Tennyson. Maybe she should start writing them down since they were beginning to add up.

She snapped off various shots, thankful for the high definition photos her new phone would provide. After Maria convinced her to upgrade her phone, she joked that the pictures showed clearer detail than she got by simply looking at something.

A few shots of the body morphed into a closeup of his hands, then his hair, and finally one of his fixed expression of surprise. He didn't appear to be someone who knew he was in shock and in danger of dying. No, he just looked startled. She needed to know what startled him.

Chapter Four

D ETECTIVE WELLS WAS the last to leave. Mark walked the man to the door, discussing what they would do the next day. The dull thunk of the deadbolt meant the inn was closed for the night and none too soon. Donna stepped into the foyer only to see her husband staring at the empty spot at the bottom of the stairs.

Even though the unfortunate Joseph Carpenter hadn't bled out on her rug, she still removed the oriental runner that had resided there. It felt tainted to her. Maybe a good cleaning might remove the psychological stain, but then again, maybe not. The rug would probably be happier somewhere else. Another owner would have no clue about its association and, in turn, no worries.

A hearty exhale escaped her lips as she joined her husband. "I'm thankful there's no yellow crime scene tape."

"Me, too. People do stupid things every day, and sometimes their actions are fatal. Still, weird about the allergic reaction. You'd think a person would know what to avoid and all."

"Yeah," she agreed as Mark placed his arm around her. The warm weight of his half-embrace had her snuggling into it. Too bad her thoughts couldn't be just as relaxed and mellow. Even though her husband could be a stickler for details, taking samples and photos for a just in case scenario, he'd eventually dismissed the unfortunate guest as just another accident.

It should be easy to put it out of her mind. After all, she had a skeleton to worry about and live guests arriving on the morrow. The one thing that helped her order her thoughts was cooking and eating, but not necessarily in that order. "I know you already had a sandwich, but that wasn't a real meal. Feel like a little snack?"

Mark pulled her tight for a little squeeze. "I thought you'd never ask. Are we talking about cheesecake?"

"Ha. You know that's not on your healthy lifestyle plan."

His arm dropped from her shoulders and he gave a dismissive snort. "I gave up smoking."

"Only after a serious heart attack."

She turned toward the kitchen and gave her husband a backward look to see if he was following. He was and complaining as he did.

"I've been walking thirty minutes every day."

"It's a start. That stroll you take with Jasper can't count as exercise. The dog stops every foot to sniff everything."

"Yeah." He shrugged. "But it's something. I even switched to decaf."

"Only after four pm." No need to add she knew he didn't adhere to that one religiously. Sometimes it was hard to do since you couldn't count on everyone going decaf with you. Still, she would have sworn when she met Mark that the man would never give up his coffee or cigarettes. He not only gave up one, he cut back on the other, and even reduced the number of desserts he consumed on a weekly basis.

Donna hated the last one because it forced her to eat less yummy concoctions or at least around her hubby. Truly, she couldn't serve her guests something she hadn't tasted herself, which resulted in a nibble here and there. Her waistline had the bad taste to bear witness to her actions. "It's been a high-stress day. I believe we both deserve some cheesecake."

"Yippee!"

The sudden shout caused Jasper to bark in response from the confines of Tennyson's room. The door must have already been open since the dog zoomed into the kitchen as he continued to yip. He made one lap around the kitchen island, then collapsed in his dog bed.

Tennyson followed much slower, scratching his head. "Hey, what's going on? Did you crack open that box from the basement and find a million dollars?"

"The box?" Good gravy! Where had she put it? Everything had happened at once.

Mark answered from his spot at the sink where he was washing his hands. "Don't worry about that. I put it away someplace safe. Didn't know if the forensic anthropologist would want to examine that, too. Personally, I don't think anything will come of the skeleton. The statute of limitation for a murder is a century. Doesn't mean our skeleton is a criminal case, probably some relative buried on the family farm. Might even be a Native American."

He put it away in a safe place? Where might that be? It was pretty obvious he didn't mention where that safe place was, so no one would get the urge to peek. The box was heavy, padlocked, and could have broken her toes when it tumbled out of her hands. She hadn't even realized Mark was nearby when she dropped it. A thick cloud of apprehension must have dulled her senses. All she really could remember was the fear that she didn't need one more dead body associated with the inn, and she didn't want to let the worker inside the inn to spot the deceased.

The only good thing about an out-of-town guest dropping dead was that the locals seldom gossiped long about someone they didn't know. There was no history for people to resurrect, simply a stranger chose to die in their community. It didn't even figure into the birth and death records since the individual wasn't a resident. Let's hope the newest death would have a short-lived gossip history. A smile tugged her lips upward as a brilliant possibility crossed her mind.

Mark swung open the freezer and peered inside. He pulled out a filled plastic bag and held it up. "Swedish meatballs. They sound good even without the noodles. I know I had a sandwich, but it was a very small sandwich." He did a double check when he noticed Donna's expression. "Hey, I know that look. Should I ask what you're thinking about?"

"You can. I thought the discovery of the skeleton would over-shadow someone tumbling down our stairs."

"Yeah, I can see that. The locals expect tourists to do stupid things, so this would only fulfill their expectations, where a skeleton is an entirely different matter. Everyone will be scratching their brains for people who have left the town over time."

It might work unless people thought she'd killed a missing resident and buried them on her property. "You make sure you let people know the skeleton was found under the foundation, which means I had nothing to do with it."

"I'll do that." He grinned and added, "You do realize gossip has nothing to do with factual information."

He was right, which only made her groan. They had some world class gossips in town, especially if she considered Eloise who didn't even need a thread of truth to create an entire story. The only good thing was people tended to avoid the woman in an effort not to be featured in her gossip commentary.

Tennyson pulled up a stool and gestured to the package of meatballs Mark still held. "I'd like some meatballs. With all the chaos in the house, all I've had to eat is the peanut butter sandwich I slapped together before the dead guy showed up."

Ah yes, she had wanted to talk to Ten about that. She held her finger up for attention, but Tennyson kept talking.

"I wouldn't worry about the skeleton. I took a peek under the inn, and all I could see was some long bones sticking out among the broken foundation. You wouldn't even know it was a human skeleton, except for the skull nearby."

Mark put the meatballs on the counter to cross his arms and directed a stern look in Ten's direction. "You didn't touch anything?"

"No. I even held Jasper back when he wanted to play with the bones."

Donna closed her eyes, not wanting to imagine her indulged pooch gallivanting around the yard with a human bone in his mouth. The snooty neighbors had never warmed up to a bed and breakfast in their vicinity. In their opinions, somehow her inn, despite the repairs she'd made to it, brought the tone of the neighborhood down. "Thank goodness."

The young employee waved their concerns away, leaned across the island surface, and confided in a conspiratorial whisper, "I think it has something to do with Herman's diamond story. The skeleton could be the victim of a double cross and the box could be—" His voice trailed off, allowing each person to speculate on the meaning.

Diamonds! Where had her husband put the box? If it was found on her property, then it had to be hers, right? Maybe, technically theirs. Even though Mark's name wasn't on the deed, they had vowed to share all their worldly goods. Her heart beat a little faster as she considered what she could do with the jewels.

People tended to visit the unique inns, those that had a little something different. There was one located in a former jail, not something she wanted to emulate. Then there were the farm ones with goats and llamas. Another thing she'd pass on. Most of the younger guests were disappointed they didn't have a pool, which might be a possibility, even though the beach was within walking distance. First, they had to build the tiny shed of a guesthouse for Mark and her. Maybe she could include a jacuzzi in the first-floor bath since it had the biggest bathroom.

Mark's voice penetrated her reverie about how she could spend her diamond money. "Should I ask if that wistful expression is due to a new kitchen appliance or our impending honeymoon?"

Her face heated, not wanting to confess her actual thoughts. "I need to get the food heated, or we'll be having a midnight supper."

Her husband's eyebrows lifted, letting her know he saw through her. That's the problem with marrying an astute man, especially one who was lied to on a regular basis. A person could be two words into an explanation for why he/she wasn't at the scene, or didn't even know the accused, and that was all Mark needed to already know if it was a lie or the truth. The hard work came in when he had to sift through the lies to pick out which line of questioning he might pursue.

Since Legacy wasn't an overly large town, the culprits were often the same, except when tourists swelled the population during prime season. A couple of senior residents felt the need to contact the police when they received inferior service at the local eateries or when the price of stamps went up. Then there were the date complaints. It wasn't anything about sexual harassment or being stalked. A few women called to complain that an online date turned out to be not as young as his photo and not as wealthy as his profile implied. They wanted to press fraud charges, but Mark would painstakingly explain that the charge wasn't relative unless a contract was signed. He felt a woman shouldn't expect to get back money spent on nails and hair, either.

The few murders that had happened were laid at the feet of out-of-towners. The few locals that contributed to a murder had their family lines traced back to when the families weren't residents, even if that meant going back a hundred years or more, which demonstrated Mark's theory that tourists were trouble. However, without them, there would be no inn, which was a sticking point.

Donna pulled out the cut raw vegetables and low-fat dip, determined to keep the meal relatively healthy. Once the food was in the toaster oven and a pot of decaf brewed, she pulled up a stool to the island. Tennyson and Mark were conversing about an upcoming beach babe beauty contest sponsored by the local radio station. Ten thought it was a good thing, but Mark saw the contest as opening the doors to their sleepy little town becoming the Key West of the North and the would-be destination of college students who wanted a wild spring break experience that they couldn't remember.

She'd heard about the contest from one of the nurses who had already filled out an application for her six-month-old baby. "Please. It's not what you think it is. It's a photo contest for babies. You can vote for the baby you like by donating money. The money raised goes back to a beach beautification fund."

Mark heaved a huge sigh while Tennyson acted like a dog who'd just been denied an anticipated treat. Sometimes men failed to get the whole story and ran with assumptions. Speaking of whole stories, it was past time to query her employee. Despite everyone's belief in their excellent memories, she discovered most people forgot fast.

"I was wondering if you remembered anything about the guy

you checked in." She angled her head in Ten's direction, although it should be self-evident whom she was talking to.

He'd picked up a celery stick and was about to bite into it as she asked. Just when she thought he'd pause to answer her inquiry, he bit into the stick instead. Donna watched him chew as slowly as she'd ever seen him chew, considering he usually inhaled food in order to eat more of it. A quick glance at her husband revealed amused eyes. Yeah, he also recognized Ten was stalling.

Donna cleared her throat, ready to restate her question when Ten audibly swallowed.

"Aw, I knew you were going to ask me that. Truth is I didn't pay that much attention to the guy. I was just irritated he showed up early. When you left you told me no one would arrive until tomorrow. I always hate checking in guests since they can be so picky. Maybe they think their room isn't on the right floor or the bed is oriented in the wrong direction. You're much better at dealing with ornery people."

Was there an unspoken inference in his statement? Perhaps he could have easily tacked on how she could handle difficult people since she could be fussy on occasions. Mark picked up the conversational thread, feeling Ten would feel less threatened by a nonemployer. They had a relationship that felt more like trusted mentor and protegee. If Mark said something, Ten not only held onto it but repeated it as if gospel.

"Do you remember how Joseph acted? Maybe his shoulders were slumped forward as if he'd just been dumped by his girlfriend."

The man was hinting at depression. It was a possibility, but no one eats something they're allergic to due to depression. Did they? Of course, Joseph could have been allergic to something else besides food.

"No. He didn't act upset." He shook his head slowly as his eyes rolled up trying to catch a fleeting impression. "I told you he had on a beanie that he had pulled down around his ears and sunglasses. He probably kept the glasses on because it was his thing."

Donna, not sure what *thing* he was talking about, shrugged, and gestured for him to continue. "Anything else?"

"Even though he had the glasses on, he acted like he owed me money or something."

Donna and Mark remarked in unison, "What?"

"You know. When someone owes you money and doesn't have it, he won't make eye contact. Instead, he kept looking around the room."

Good description, but it didn't answer her initial thought that the man was already going into shock. Maybe he just needed a room, and he'd administer his own epinephrine. "Could you tell if he was flushed, sweating, puffy?"

Ten shoved one hand through his hair. "I never saw the guy before in my life." Ten shook his head and continued in a softer voice. "I don't ogle guys."

Donna expected as much since her employee was probably one of the least confrontational persons she knew. Too often men regarded a direct stare by another man as aggressive, especially when the person was unknown. Family members and friends could get away with it, most of the time. Still, it was hard imagining her guest checking in without looking up. There had to be eye contact at some time.

"When I cut off the mask, you mentioned you weren't sure if it was the same guy."

The toaster oven buzzer went off, but Donna stared at Ten, willing him to recall that moment. He was young and couldn't use the excuse that his memory wasn't what it used to be. She had read the younger set didn't try to memorize events or even facts, though, knowing they could always use their smartphones for that. Some didn't even know their own phone number.

Mark got up with a murmur, something about the food drying out while she had a standoff. The metallic creak of the toaster oven door meant he was retrieving the nibbles.

Tennyson wiggled his chin one way then another, before speaking. "I said that?"

Donna nodded in encouragement, afraid words might stop him. Mark called out from the other side of the kitchen. "Why? What was different? Take your time."

One hand went to her hip as she twisted around to regard her husband. What was he doing? Hijacking her question? The questions did have the desired result, though.

"The dude on the floor looked shorter."

That may not be as helpful information as it seemed since Tennyson topped over six foot and he was standing, looking down at a prone figure, which would make anyone look smaller or shorter.

"Anything else?" she interjected, afraid Mark might get the jump on her again.

His brows knitted together, before he held up one finger. "He looked pale when I saw him on the floor. Do you think he was flushed when he came in?"

That was one possibility. Another one was once the heart stops working, the blood drains from the skin and puddles at the lowest area making the individual look lighter. So far, he hadn't given her any great clues. The man may have been in shock, but she couldn't understand him not being aware of it.

Back when she was in middle-school, a classmate had died from eating a fund-raising chocolate bar chock-full of nuts. Personally, she couldn't understand why her parents even let her carry around something that could be dangerous to her. As she recalled, the girl speculated on how the bar would taste and how people appeared to enjoy it. She could eat chocolate, but not nuts and wondered aloud if she were truly allergic. Even back then, Donna could be a bit officious and had reminded her that if the doctors told her she was allergic, she must be.

The fateful day happened when Donna was doing research in the library. Sometimes she fantasized that if she had been there she could have recognized the signs. The other students explained she had eaten the candy bar before lunch because she was hungry. By the time the ambulance arrived, she was dead. This was back before people carried epi pens around with them to deal with allergic reactions. The epinephrine in the pen stimulated the heart, constricted the blood vessels to improve blood pressure, and relaxed the smooth muscles in the lungs for easier breathing.

Did the man not have a pen or make the mistake of thinking he didn't need one? An unneeded injection would cause a racing heart, general jitteriness, and possible headache. Someone with a possible heart condition ran the risk of going into cardiac arrest. The more she thought about it the more questions she had.

Mark carried the food to the island and passed out plates and silverware. The men helped themselves to the meatballs but bypassed the veggies. Knowing he couldn't have missed the colorful veggies, Donna pushed them closer to Mark's plate. He took a few carrots. *It was a start.* She scooped meatballs onto her plate and added green pepper strips on the side when another question occurred to her.

"When are they going to do the autopsy?"

Ten choked on what he was eating. Donna administered a hearty slap on his back, her eyes on his flushed face for signs she might need to administer the Heimlich maneuver. He waved her away, having already experienced the maneuver on a previous occasion.

"I'm okay as long as you don't mention cutting people open while I'm eating."

Mark chuckled, probably because he could talk about anything while wolfing down a pound of meatballs and black coffee. "I doubt there will be an autopsy. You heard Oscar. The man had an allergic reaction, then tumbled down the stairs. End of story. His people can come for him, take him to whatever funeral home they want, and ask for an autopsy then."

She'd never know if an autopsy was performed and what the results were if it was done elsewhere. "Funeral homes do that now?"

"If they have a licensed pathologist and an autopsy technician, which many of the larger chains do."

Tennyson moaned and pushed his uneaten meatballs away. "You two can ruin a nice meal. Didn't anyone teach you to converse about something that would interest everyone?"

Ah yes, her mother did. Strange that her mother's sentiments came out of her employee's mouth. Mother took an interest in Tennyson and regarded him as a foster grandchild. It would be like her to instruct him in simple etiquette. This would give her mother another chance after she appeared to have failed with Donna and her brother, Daniel. At least neither one of them chewed with their mouths open.

Jasper lifted his head, his nose quivering, somehow aware there might be a meatball or two in his future. The dog had ESP when it came to food. He made a show of slowly getting to all four feet and ambling toward the island where Tennyson fed him a meatball.

Since Ten stopped eating, it was a green light to continue her conversation. "Would there be any reason for you to obtain a copy of the autopsy?"

"No." His bushy eyebrows went up in inquiry.

Of course, he sensed the direction she was traveling. The man was a detective, after all. Trying to distract him from her obvious belief that the death wasn't as accidental as it seemed and her ploy to get proof, she concentrated on his eyebrows.

"Donna, I'm not getting them waxed as some of the other guys at the station are doing. Next time I'm at the barber I'll get them trimmed."

"Did I say anything?"

"Not outright, but you keep staring at them."

Goodness. "That was rude of me."

"True. That's one of the reasons I love you. Too often, women want to play all these guessing games where men are supposed to automatically know what they want. When they don't, they're accused of not caring. Not you. You're an easy read even when you're not talking."

It was fortunate she fell in love with a man who appreciated her no-nonsense attitude and outspokenness. Mark could be a bit of a know-it-all, too. Every now and then she liked to test his deductive skills. "What am I thinking now?"

"How lucky you are to have married me."

He hit that nail on the head. His eyes twinkled, probably because her mouth dropped open with his pronouncement.

"You're also worried that your deceased guest was murdered."

Sometimes it was frustrating that he could be right almost all the time. "You're good. There's no denying it. Sometimes I wish I could just sneak something by you."

His shoulders went up in a shrug. "Not sure why you would. Go ahead and try. I will warn you that you have tells. Everyone does."

"I do. What are they?"

"Nope." He folded his arms and grinned. "If I told you that would remove the element of sportsmanship. Your brother chuckles before he decides to tell a whopper."

"I was the one who told you that."

"True." He shrugged but refused to say anymore.

She was not sure how sportsmanlike it was having an advantage over another person. If she had any tells, surely her mother would know since she'd never successfully lied as a child. Her mother always knew. She waved her hand in his direction. "Don't tell me. I bet I can fool you. Your challenge is accepted."

Even as she said the overconfident words, Donna accepted that it would be hard to fool her ever-observant husband. The best thing to do was to give him hints or accidental slips about something she wasn't planning to do. The man thought she couldn't keep a secret. He was in for a surprise.

Chapter Five

SOMETHING NIBBLED AT Donna's dreams, pushing itself into the one that featured her telling smiling workmen about the waterfall she wanted in her pool. It would make for some great online promotional pictures. Who didn't want a waterfall pool? Possibly those who didn't want to be bothered with the upkeep. Maybe that explained the uncomfortable feeling that had her tossing and turning in bed. Mark's elbow in her back pushed her from her slumber and had her blinking into the darkness.

Had her husband elbowed her on purpose? No, he would have been more likely to have shaken her awake and asked what was wrong. A half-roll allowed her to see the glowing red numerals of her bedside clock. The numbers glared back at her as if daring her into some type of action. No one should be awake at three-thirty in the morning with the exception of shift workers.

Her head flopped back onto the pillow. If she knew what woke her, she might be able to get back to sleep. The jingle of Jasper's dog tags meant he was awake, which meant he'd want to go out. Donna slid out of bed carefully, not wanting to wake Mark. A continuous snore assured her she hadn't.

Jasper's nails clicked across the wood floor whenever he veered off the thick oriental rug. The bottom globe of the hurricane lamp glowed in the hallway, allowing her to move freely toward the kitchen. She smiled as she passed it thinking it felt so much friendlier than a nightlight stuck in an outlet. Her bare feet encountered the wood floor, baffling her for a moment until she remembered she'd removed the runner that had led to the steps.

What she forgot to do came barreling straight at her. She'd never checked the late Joseph Carpenter's room. It was hard to believe she forgot in the chaos. Surely, Mark had, especially considering Detective Wells had dropped by. Still, she lingered at the foot of the stairs looking upwards. Wells could have been there on some non-police related matter since he was buying Mark's house.

Jasper nudged her hand reminding her that she still hadn't let him out. She'd better do that first. They both moved silently through the kitchen, past Tennyson's room where she could still hear the television playing low, which meant he probably fell asleep with it on again.

Outside, Donna waited in the warm summer air, turning slowly to locate the moon. To her left and not quite full, there was an ominous red cast to it. There used to be some saying about the moon. "Red sky at night, sailors' delight. Red sky in the morning, sailors take warning."

Not it. Maybe there weren't any sayings about a blood moon. Her nose wrinkled, not liking the way *blood moon* sounded, even in her mind. It could be a rose moon or a red moon, something a tad more cheerful. It could even be a cherry moon.

Jasper, done with his business, mounted the steps, wagging his tail. Half the time, Donna wondered if he ever did anything besides have a walk around and sniff everything. His main goal was to get the dog treat she provided when he came in at night. It certainly was an easier system than searching the yard for her dog in the dark or yelling for him in the wee hours, which would have earned her zero points with her neighbors.

Once she locked the door after Jasper, she knew it was time to check the room. A quick search through the kitchen cabinet netted her the flashlight she needed. It would be better not to turn on lights until she at least made it to the second floor, not wanting to wake Mark. As she ascended the stairs, the familiar jingle of dog tags meant Jasper was determined to accompany her. He'd probably give up by the second-floor landing since he was no fan of stairs.

At the landing, she turned on a light in the pantry lounge for Jasper before hitting the second set of stairs. She used the bright beam from the flashlight to illuminate the steps. The overhead lights would work so much better, but they'd light up the foyer.

She was in her own inn and knew every inch of it, except for the skeleton in the foundation part. Make that she knew every cleanable inch of it. Still, creeping around in the middle of the night with a flashlight while everyone else was asleep rated creepy.

On the third landing, she turned on the light and took a deep breath. Those stairs took it out of her. When she had her breath back, another epiphany occurred—she didn't have the key to the room. *Good gravy.*

Wait. Tennyson may have given the early guest a key, but no one returned one. Come to think of it, she wasn't even sure what room was his. Talk about a pointless adventure in the night. Since she was already there, she should try the doors.

The first was one locked, which meant nothing. The second one didn't budge, either. The third was her last hope before trudging back down the stairs and grabbing all the third story keys. The doorknob turned easily under her hand. Success!

Aha, who's the master sleuth now! Her eyes dropped to her hand, which still gripped the knob. There might have been fingerprints on the doorknobs other than her own. Just Joseph Carpenter's though, which wouldn't have been that big of a surprise.

Inside the room, she flicked on the light. The bathroom looked clean, undisturbed, except the toilet lid was up, indicating a male had recently used it. There was also a slight impression on the bed comforter, which meant Joseph had sat there briefly.

Nothing else. More importantly, there wasn't a single piece of luggage. All Tennyson appeared to notice was that the man carried a large unicorn mask. Since she'd coached her employee to carry luggage to the guest's room, he would have focused on a suitcase since it meant both extra work and a tip. Weird.

When Mark awoke, she'd ask him if he took anything from the room. She hadn't recalled Mark going up the stairs. Donna went back to the door, pretending she was Joseph. The symptoms of anaphylactic shock due to an extreme allergic reaction included feeling hot, itching, sweating, nausea, and dizziness.

She staggered a little bit, pretending to be Joseph and grabbed at the bathroom doorway as she lurched through the door. It wasn't unusual for someone to vomit or have diarrhea while in shock since the body was trying to rid itself of the toxin. The seat position made no sense for either. The little triangle she made with the tissue still remained. Obviously, the man was well enough at that point to stand upright.

When had he become so sick he decided to don a mask and stroll around? The small indent on the bed was more the type made by someone momentarily perching on the bed. Someone in full-scale shock would have collapsed on the bed immediately. The more she knew the less anything made sense.

Donna turned out the light and made the decision to come back to lock the door. Thank goodness she had made several keys for the room, since the one Tennyson must have handed over was nowhere to be found.

Most people would point out that a lost key meant nothing. Yeah, but add a lost key to an upright toilet seat, and a butt impression in the bed, and it meant something. Her lips pursed as she considered, it could mean that Tennyson had cleaned the room. She didn't mind him using the room toilet as he cleaned if only he'd put the seat down. No one wanted to see a seat up when first checking in. It gave the implication the room hadn't been cleaned. As for the bed, he could have paused a moment to check his phone.

She was already at the landing when she remembered the wardrobe in the bedroom. Houses built when the inn was often didn't include closets. If they did have closets they were less than a foot deep and resembled more of a cabinet. It had something to do with the houses being taxed on how many rooms they had and a closet was counted as a room.

What if there was something important in the wardrobe that she missed? A tired voice floated up the stairwell.

"Donna? What are you doing roaming about in the middle of the night?"

Oops! It was Mark, and she hadn't meant to wake him. He'd turned on the stairwell lights, making it easier to find her way. She hurried down the stairs not wanting to yell her reply. A bleary-eyed husband stood on the second-floor landing with Jasper beside him. Her canine glanced away when she reached the two, giving her a clue to who woke whom.

"Hey, I didn't want to wake you."

Mark yawned and managed a tired smile. "I figured as much, but you didn't pass on the word to your pooch. He scratched at the door wanting to get back in."

The glare she directed at her canine was ignored as her dog

turned and made his own way down the stairs. Probably figured his job was done since both humans were now up. Her husband reached for her hand as they watched Jasper turn the corner and disappear into the foyer. Mark squeezed her hand and asked, "Should I assume you were sleuthing?"

"Some."

"Find anything?"

"Not really. No room key. Toilet seat in an odd position, the bed had been sat on, but no luggage."

"Nothing sounds that peculiar."

Donna cleared her throat. "Did you miss the *no* luggage?"

"I had Wells retrieve a single carry-on, and he took it to the coroner's. Whoever comes for the body will want the suitcase."

Yeah, that made sense. There was also the possibility that Wells could have used the toilet while upstairs. It looked like she had no information except for her missing room key. "You could have told me this, so I wasn't sneaking around in the middle of the night."

The hand holding hers dropped and wrapped around her waist, pulling her closer. Mark dusted a kiss across her sleep-mussed hair. "I would have if you'd asked. Let's see if we can catch some Z's before morning comes.

DONNA WAS ALREADY in the kitchen brewing coffee when Maria and Baby Cici arrived. She smiled at the newest arrivals, always happy to see her niece, but even happier to see a pair of extra, competent hands in the form of her sister-in-law. Maria would have no issue with looking guests in the eyes and telling them no if they over-reached with their demands. The thought made her chuckle.

The dark-eyed beauty rested the child on one hip as she slung the baby bag and purse on the counter. "What's so funny, especially at this time of the morning?"

Another chuckle escaped before she could get her breath to explain. She held one finger up signaling her to wait. "Okay," she managed to declare once she caught her breath. "Just had a sudden funny. As you know, I've been working on being a kinder, politer innkeeper, which involves me not saying what I'd like to say with so many souls out there that need my guidance."

Maria hoisted one eyebrow and sat Baby Cici on the island, possibly breaking several health code violations in doing so. "Daniel and I have enjoyed watching you struggle with that aspect of the business. Not sure why you would find it funny."

The baby on the island would have to be addressed, but instead of mentioning it immediately, Donna grabbed some disinfectant wipes. A playpen in the kitchen might offer a nice alternative, especially considering the majority of her work took place there. She edged closer to the island waiting for Maria to pick up the baby. The purse and bag were probably even more germy since they didn't receive a daily bath.

"It's not my constant struggle to not speak the truth that amused me. I thought I might be rubbing off on you. Instead of being your super sweet self, I've noticed you've been more assertive with the paying guests in not letting them make unreasonable requests as they did before."

"I haven't changed, not really." She nodded at the wipes in Donna's hand and picked up Cici. "Before, you would have told me how germy my child was, but now you're the one hovering, waiting to swoop in without a word."

My goodness, Maria had a point. Donna had changed some. "Well, you used to make up all those regulations to force guests to comply. What happened with that?"

"Got tired of making them up. Besides, you have your closet rebels who want to test regulations just to see if some person in a cheap suit with identification will show up and call them on it. Most are assured they won't. I decided to go with the no-nonsense approach. No, you can't have breakfast in bed, but it's available in the dining room between nine and ten."

Yeah, that worked for her. When Donna did it, she was called rude. It helped to be young and gorgeous. With a smile, Maria could calmly inform some of the guests they had no running water, and they'd accept it.

"You can get away with that. I can't. Once I got started I'd be telling them no shoes on the bed, not to remove makeup with our washcloths, and not to open the windows since it messes with the air conditioning." Donna took the opportunity while her niece was held, to remove the bags to the stool, and wipe down the island. "I can pick up a playpen for her."

"No need. Cecilia already bought one for the inn. Tennyson can bring it in."

Sounded like her mother, always one step ahead of everyone. "I'm surprised she didn't have it delivered."

"She did, but not to the inn. One of the delivery people left it on our porch. When I swung the door open there it was. It was a bear to wrestle into my small car."

"Let's give Ten the honors of toting it in and unpacking it."

As if on cue, a sleepy looking Tennyson strolled into the kitchen rubbing at his pillow-creased face. "Did I hear my name?"

Her sister-in-law shot him a brilliant smile while Donna explained, "We need you to go get the playpen out of Maria's car."

He gave a heavy put-out sigh before turning toward the back

door. Jasper, her puggle, trailed after him, wagging his tail. She waited until the door closed before grinning. Every day that went by made Tennyson seem more like a family member as opposed to an employee. "He's a good kid."

"Yeah, you're lucky to have him."

"I had my doubts at first when he wanted to know what type of cable package I had."

"You need to remember room and board is not the prize it used to be with plenty of millennials deciding to live with their parents indefinitely."

Shouting outside cut off any reply she might have made. Donna rushed to the back door, still clutching the wipes container to hear Tennyson's shout.

"Get away from there! This is private property. You're trespassing!"

What could be happening now? Donna stepped out into the bright early morning light only to see Ten waving his arms at fleeing figures. Jasper barked hard, not necessarily concerned about defending the property, but anxious to have his say.

The tiny excavator the elevator company used sat beside some lumber and a portable cement mixer. A blue tarp was stapled over the area still under construction. Donna picked her way across the yard, avoiding the raised roots of the older trees. She'd learned her lesson the first time when she took a flying fall when chasing an intruder.

Tennyson walked slowly back to where Donna stood by the excavator. He murmured to himself, something along the lines of nosy kids. Even the tone of his voice, mixed with a tiny bit of frustration and irritation, reminded her so much of Mark that she had to fight the urge to smirk.

"Ten! What happened?"

He gave a derisive snort. "Neighborhood geniuses decided to check out the skeleton. Gossip spreads fast in this town."

It did.

"Did they get in? Grab anything?" All she needed was some bones improperly removed to bring down some curse on her inn. Not that she believed any of that nonsense, but why take chances?

Instead of answering, the lanky employee moved to the blue tarp and tugged at the edges. "No. It's still stapled in place. After I had my peek at the bones yesterday, another worker stapled the area closed with a doubled tarp to prevent entry."

A twinge twitched at the base of her neck. Probably guilt making an appearance, reminding her she should have inspected the area as opposed to spending all her time on her unicorn masked guest. Personally, she thought one crisis a day was plenty. Too bad the fates didn't schedule accordingly. "Good deal. Right now, I just want the skeleton to be gone. A forensic paleontologist is supposed to be coming today."

"Cool. Is it going to be like that television show? Will the FBI show up, too?"

Maybe that's what the local teens thought and were anxious to get in on the action. At least no one had slipped in under the cover of night. Jasper sniffed around the tarp, forcing her to redirect her dog with a gentle nudge of her foot. The teens might have been chased away with a shout, but not Jasper, who would burrow under the tarp with ease.

"No FBI. There's no crime. I guess calling in a paleontologist is standard practice when you uncover old bones, especially when you don't know who they belong to."

Ten gave her a head bob that reminded her so much of Mark she could have sworn the boy had been practicing it, but she doubted it. When people spent enough time around others, they often picked up on their traits, which explained why her father steered her away from screeching playmates at a young age.

Usually, when Mark bobbed his head in that manner, it meant he was humoring her and not convinced of whatever theory she was espousing at the time. "There's nothing to the bones. Probably an old family grave."

Ten gave the blue tarp a suspicious glance. "It could be. It might be one of those guardians. People used to kill a person and bury them on the property to watch over it and scare off any intruders."

Her eyebrows arched as she wrinkled her nose at the suggestion. The boy needed to improve his reading or at least his late-night television viewing. "There's so much wrong with your guardian theory. Why would anyone want to watch over someone's property who just killed them?"

"I wondered about that. Maybe they volunteered?"

Her lips pressed into a firm line, telling how she felt about the possibility. "I need to get breakfast started and do a final check on the rooms before I head to the hospital. You need to get the playpen. We'll leave the back door open to listen if our bone snoops return."

Donna strolled back to the inn, and Tennyson fell into step behind her but veered off to the parking lot. What she didn't hear was the jingle of Jasper's dog tags. Dagnabit, her pooch was up to no good. She turned in time to see her dog lifting his leg in the direction of the tarp.

She should have suspected as much. Jasper was claiming it for his own. A sharp whistle had her dog trotting reluctantly to the house. The paleontologist couldn't get here fast enough.

The coffee aroma lured her to the carafe. Maria sat at the island with the laptop booted up and Baby Cici on her lap. "Have you seen the Gen Con schedule?"

"I've been a little busy with a recently dead body and a long ago dead skeleton."

"Never mind. I'll print it out. I'm sure the guests will want copies. There's going to be a miniature display at the convention center. There's a Dungeon and Dragons tournament. Also, signups for various LARP games."

"Lark?" Donna poured herself a cup of coffee as she puzzled over the idea of a game being a lark.

Maria looked up from the laptop to explain. "LARP stands for live action role-playing games. People dress up like the characters in the game and act it out."

Donna's eyes narrowed. "You mean to tell me someone wants to dress up like that top-hat wearing guy from Monopoly?"

"Maybe, but most will be from adventure games, some board, some video. There's a real industry providing costumes for them. I even heard there's a factory in China that does nothing but make costumes for role-playing games. Costumed role play is called cosplay."

Donna shook her head. "It's disco all over again."

Maria twisted around on the stool, keeping a firm hold on the newest Tollhouse. "What are you talking about?"

The clang of the pans served as the prelude for breakfast as Donna centered two skillets on the burners. "It's just going to be bacon and eggs since no guests are here."

"Sounds good to me. What do costumes have to do with disco?"

Donna chuckled as she pulled the bacon and a carton of eggs out of the fridge. "I keep forgetting how young you are. Back when disco was popular, it was a time for people to try out different personalities. The shy wallflower could don a wig and some shades and become a dancing queen. People showed up in everything from feathers to boy scout uniforms."

Maria cupped the baby's hand and had her point in Donna's direction. In a high voice representing the baby, Maria spoke, "I can't believe you ever dressed up as someone else and went to the disco."

"Those were different times. There was no game playing involved unless you included the lies people told one another when trying to score a date."

"That's still the same."

The bacon strip Donna lowered into the skillet sizzled on contact. She placed another strip in the pan while considering her sister-in-law's last remark. "I count myself lucky to have caught the last decent man in Legacy."

It wouldn't take the bacon very long to cook, so she moved on to the eggs. She took two eggs in one hand with the intention of cracking them into the skillet, when she saw a shadowy form in the back hallway.

"Aw!" She jumped back in surprise, dropping the eggs on the floor.

Mark stepped all the way into the kitchen. "I didn't mean to scare you."

Not willing to admit the sight of a shadowy figure had her thinking about guardian nonsense, she threw her husband a narrow-eyed glance. "I wasn't scared."

Maria stared down at the yolky mess on the floor. "Those eggs say different."

Everybody was a comedian. Only, it wasn't funny, and she'd have to clean it up. She reached for the large box of table salt and liberally coated the goo, drying it up enough to sweep into a dustpan.

Her eyes found the culprit of the egg drop. "Why did you sneak in on us like that?"

"Obviously to hear good things about myself." He walked over to Donna and dusted a kiss across her cheek. "Let me clean this up. It only seems fair since I inadvertently caused it."

The man took the blame when he deserved it and knew what to do to make it right. "I know you didn't come back from the station to see if we'd gossip about you."

Broom in hand, Mark walked toward the salt concentration and kept his eyes down. "I thought I might drop by and deliver my news, personally."

Here it comes. She sagged against the nearby cabinet. "I should have suspected something. Go ahead. Make like it's a Band-Aid and rip it off. What's happening?"

"The paleontologist needs a room and every place is filled due to Gen Con. There are dozens of RVs at the fairgrounds and a few have even set up tents."

She pursed her lips, wondering how to accommodate the woman when a bell went off over her head. "She can have Joseph Carpenter's room. It would be cool, though, if no one mentioned the former guest dying. People can be weird about stuff like that."

"Maybe Dr. Haddox won't since she works with bones, but where some people are cool with ghosts, they get freaked out over the recently departed. It's great you have a room for her, but what are we going to do about her assistants?"

She wanted to suggest a tent, considering it was summer. "Aren't people in that field used to living out in the open?"

"I think you are talking about archeologists and that's only a small part of their lives. I imagine even a graduate student is used to more than a grass bed."

Mark had given her a dilemma—one she was determined to solve.

Chapter Six

I N ORDER TO accommodate Dr. Haddox and her graduate student assistants, Mark and Donna decided to relocate to his house that was undergoing painting to get rid of the stale cigarette smell. There were drop cloths everywhere and a ladder right in the middle of the hallway. Donna worked her way around the painting paraphernalia and into the first bedroom stacked with boxes.

A closed window served as her goal as she stepped around cartons marked *charity* and another few had KEEP written in capital letters. It almost made her stop to peek inside, but the paint fumes urged her on. A few tugs on the window finally released the grip time had had on the frame. It made her wonder if her sweetie had ever opened the windows in his home. That would depend on him being home, and she knew the man had worked long hours before he met her. His schedule still kept him busy, but at least she saw him in the mornings before he left and when he came home.

Summer had descended upon Legacy with a vengeance, which meant no refreshing breeze came through the screen window. The air was still and hot, the same as the interior, except the smell of cut grass dominated the outside.

"Donna! Where are you?"

"In here!"

"Where's here?"

Mark's voice sounded closer. The suburban ranch was an older model with only three bedrooms and one bathroom. It was built back before people discovered two bathrooms were a must.

As a bachelor, Mark never had a need for another bathroom. Her lips pursed as she debated about asking if any woman ever shared his house. Her mother maintained part of a happy relationship was knowing the questions not to ask. Previous loves fell under that heading.

"I'm in the bedroom with all the boxes."

A hoarse chuckle echoed in the hallway. "That could be any of them."

"It has a desk."

Mark stood in the doorway and gestured to the room with one hand. "You're in my office."

"I so could tell. What's in all the boxes?"

One hand shot through his hair as he cleared his throat. "Good question."

The man had to be teasing her. In the beginning of their relationship, she hadn't been used to his playful nature and became defensive when she took all of his remarks seriously. "You must know what is in these boxes since you packed them."

"Thirty years. That's what's in the boxes. I've lived in this house for that long. Other than that, I'd be hard-pressed to tell you. I'm trying to pack up when I have a minute or two, but as you know we had a murder, a wedding, had to drive our senior citizen escapees back to the home, and now, Gen Con."

When put that way, it was a reasonable excuse. There were a lot of boxes. "I could help you decide what to keep."

He winked at her. "I have no doubt you could. I didn't want to burden you with this since you were already so busy selling your house, planning the wedding, and everything else."

She reached for his hand and interlaced her fingers with his. "As married folks, we are a team. I'd be glad to help you."

Mark gave her hand a slight squeeze. "I'll take you up on your offer, but first we need to square away the bedroom and turn on the air so we have some place to sleep tonight."

"We have to get that extra cot you have, too, since Dr. Haddox has two assistants. We also need to get this done before I report to work." The problem with her hospital job is it kept her out of the inn doings much of the time. She had to depend on Tennyson, Maria, and even her mother to help. It was hard for it to be her baby, when so many other people were putting their mark on the inn. Her mother had moved some furniture under the guise of getting things back to normal after the wedding. If they had taken off for a honeymoon right away, there might have been more unapproved changes.

"We'll get it done, I'll even drive you to work with the sirens blaring to get there faster."

That sounded like a possibility. At best, it would cut fifteen minutes off her commute. "You can do that?"

He shook his head. "No, I can't. The new commissioner would not approve, and I'm not ready to retire yet."

"Figured as much."

At her hospital job, she'd listen to nurses gripe about the doctors. When she visited her patients, they'd complain about the food, the doctors, and the nurses, all while she'd be stuck, having no clue what was happening at her inn. Her life's direction could be changing during the time she recorded vitals and took supper orders. The whole situation chafed. She needed to be at the inn, watching over this mysterious Dr. Haddox. The image of an officious woman with a brittle manner and reading glasses perched on her nose took shape. Who knows what she might do?

"Why do you think she needs two assistants? How long is this going to take anyhow? What if they declare the inn is some type of sacred burial ground?" Her voice grew higher and tighter with each question.

Mark pulled her into a hug and rested his head on hers. "Relax."

She took a deep breath, letting it out slowly while he spoke.

"Sure, it's inconvenient, but it won't take forever. I talked to the elevator construction foreman and outside of the elevator box and firming the foundation footing, there isn't anything else to do. They can have it done in a day."

That was supposed to be how long it would take to have put the elevator in originally. Donna had her doubts even when she received the estimate. Having a brother in construction taught her that estimates were more about what the potential customer wanted to hear and had nothing to do with reality.

It had been such a long road to her bed and breakfast, and now it felt like it was slipping away. The only reason she sold her home was to devote herself completely to the inn. Technically, she'd resigned her job at the hospital, as well, but the wily personnel manager convinced her to stay until they found a replacement. So far, no nurses were chomping at the bit to work the second shift. Some people would have chucked it, not caring if the nurses were stretched to the limit. Having worked over two decades with some, she couldn't just leave them without appropriate personnel for the workload. Then there was the issue with the second mortgage she took out initially for the improvements. Mark hadn't signed up to shoulder the financial load. He'd do it without complaint, but that wasn't the point.

Donna nuzzled into Mark's shoulder and inhaled the comforting smell of his cotton shirt and spicy aftershave. "I hope so. What do you mean there was nothing else?"

He released his embrace and stepped back to look at her. His hand cupped her chin, bringing her gaze to his. "You've read enough history books and even subscribed to the National Geographic Channel."

Her initial anxiety had eased, and her regular personality asserted itself. "Would you cut to the chase?"

He arched his eyebrows and wrinkled his nose but continued as if never interrupted. "Most cultures, especially Native Americans, buried their dead with great ceremony. They would be wrapped up in ceremonial robes. Hunting spears, pottery bowls, or any other item that was precious and possibly useful in the next life was placed in the grave."

"What about the box?" It seemed obvious to her that important things could be buried in the box. Before Mark could reply, she answered her own question. "The padlock as we know it was invented in the nineteenth century by a Swedish guy."

"How do you know that?"

"Trivia show. I only had the briefest look at the box before it tumbled to the ground. You saw it. Do you think it was a regular padlock?"

"Pretty much. I carried it to my car and put it in the trunk for safe keeping, but I did notice the lock. It was old, heavy, and possibly cast iron. Thick, too. Not sure what device we'll need to cut it off."

Donna took a step back as her hand found purchase on her hip. She regarded her husband with a speculative glance. "You've had the box in your car this entire time?"

"I'm not sure why you're acting like a scalded cat. It hasn't even been twenty-four hours, and I did put it up for safe keeping.

Already, we've had inquisitive teens snooping around the inn. Can you imagine what would have happened if I hadn't taken immediate precautions? That's why I locked it up."

"You're right." She had to agree, which bugged a little since she hadn't thought of this first. If Herman still lived across the street, he'd swear the missing diamonds were inside. She smirked, suspecting Mark would find such a claim ridiculous.

An audible gulp sounded, she looked at Mark, who didn't appear rattled and realized it must have been her. Maybe they were in the box. The possibility caused a tingle to start at her fingertips and spread throughout her body. They could fly first class on their honeymoon. Wherever that might be. The prospect of being ushered onto a jet first tempted, along with the extra leg room and the waiting water bottles for the first-class guests. Back in coach she was lucky to get half a glass of water. The stewards sometimes didn't even make it to her seat if it was a short flight or they had demanding passengers ahead of her. That had happened more than once. Those few who could afford the front of the plane had their own attendant. The siren call of sitting in first class with wider seats and the hint of being somehow better than those who flew coach seduced her. "Could we keep the diamonds?"

"What diamonds?" He cleared his throat, then his hand went to his chin, his classic thinking pose. "I assume you think there are diamonds in the box." At her emphatic nod, he gave her wink. "What would we do with the diamonds?"

"Sell them, I guess."

"Who would we sell them to?"

Donna shrugged. "I'm no jeweler. How would I know these things?"

"Diamonds are accompanied by paperwork, telling what country they came from and such. It's part of the Kimberly process to show the diamonds aren't being used to fund violence. Anyone trying to sell diamonds without the proper paperwork is suspicious. Some stones are distinctive and easily recognizable. More recently, diamonds are tattooed with tiny laser marks as a form of identification. Resourceful jewel thieves travel to countries that cut diamonds to have them recut without the mark before attempting to sell them."

"Goodness." Donna dropped the hand on her hip and splayed it against her chest. "I had no clue that Legacy was the diamond heist capital of the states."

"Go ahead and joke, but I like to keep up on current crime trends. Maybe I was influenced by all the shows featuring jewel thieves. Most people imagine themselves as the thief, but I always saw myself as the person who caught the culprit."

"Of course, you did." She inhaled deeply. It looked like her life of luxury was slipping away. "Maybe the insurance company might give us some sort of finder's fee."

"They could. You talk like the diamonds are a done deal. It's more likely the box was an early form of a fire safe full of papers that could be of interest to the local historical society."

Yeah, it was probably the latter. "One of Legacy's earlier citizens must have been beside himself not knowing where he put that darn box. We need more details. Where exactly did they find the bones?" She held up her finger, knowing what he probably would say. "Don't tell me. Under the foundation. That I know."

"I see you're in a mood. Hungry?"

She wasn't in a mood. Okay, maybe she was approaching the prelude to a mood. What woman wouldn't be with everything she had on her plate. *Wait.* A smile tipped her lips as another thought occurred at Mark's suggestion. "I am hungry. Let's grab the cot, turn on the air, and I'll let you take me out to lunch at the new place on main that everyone is talking about. Fresh delicious food served fast."

Mark shoved his hands into his pants pockets and rattled his car keys, probably trying to recall when he suggested lunch out. "Let's do it. Close that window you just opened. The cot is in the garage. You can turn on the air, and I'll meet you back out at the car."

"I'm on it." She slammed the window shut, twisted the lock, then pushed the air temp to sixty-eight. She sprinted into the bedroom and stripped off the sheets. No telling how long they had been on. Might as well take them back to the inn and launder them.

Donna rolled the sheets into a ball and stood for a moment. Even though Mark's and her relationship had spanned a few years, most of it had taken place at the inn. She'd only been in his house a handful of times. On her first visit, she remarked that it smelled like an ashtray in a train station or something equally critical. Mark could have made a conscious effort not to have her visit his home. She'd only stopped by a few times with soup when he was under the weather after that.

The faded wallpaper had squares of bright paper where photos once were. The furniture was a traditional colonial bedroom suite in maple. A television balanced on top of a dresser. The closet door was open, revealing plenty of shirts and slacks still on hangers. Donna perched on the bed, her hand on the mattress. Had Mark thought of her right before he went to sleep? Had he struggled with the idea of getting involved with her or maybe even the whole idea of commitment?

The bang of the back-screen door abruptly ended her reflection. A few hurried footsteps brought Mark into the room.

"Are you okay?" He rushed to sit by her on the bed and took her hand.

Wasn't that sweet? He was worried about her. "I'm fine. I guess I was sitting here wondering if you ever had doubts about me? Or us?"

He brought her hand to his lips and dusted a kiss across it before answering. "Never."

That seemed highly unlikely, but she'd take it. "Good. I'm ready to go."

"Me, too." Mark stood first, but Donna vaulted off the bed before he could assist her. "What was that about?"

"Nothing," No way would she tell him that her friend Janice told her you weren't truly old as long as you could get up on your own without any assistance. Aging was different for men. Plenty of middle-aged men married sweet young things and went on to beget more children. When a woman hit fifty, it was almost like a sign was placed on her. She wasn't too sure what the sign read but it might be *obsolete* or *out of order*. It was as if society didn't know what to do with women her age, especially the ones who weren't mothers.

"I have a plan I think you're going to like." He kept his grip on her hand and led her through the house.

"Tell me."

"Let's get in the car first."

Why the car? Since they had no reason to stay any longer, she complied instead of asking. Donna climbed into the front seat while Mark locked up the house. He ducked into the car with a grin and turned the engine over.

She waited until they were on their way to lunch before prodding him with her finger. "What's up?"

He pushed away her prodding finger, then gave her a sly glance.

"Have you ever done anything really naughty?"

Mercy. He hadn't been on that app Janice had told her about where people shared their darkest secrets to total strangers. She had tried it once at her friend's urging and confessed that she mocked one of the most demanding doctors behind his back. The other nurses thought she really nailed the impersonation. Still, there was no way he could know. "Are we talking about two desserts or snooping through people's stuff?"

"I already know you do both those things."

The arrangement of items in a room, and taking photos of said items, fell under investigation, or at least that is how she explained it to herself. The desserts were all part of becoming a better cook and the fact she wanted them. "Why did you ask?"

"Have you ever played hooky from work?"

"I've switched days with other nurses, which isn't actually hooky."

The turn signal clicked on as he switched lanes. "I know that. Have you ever called in for a mental health day or even treated yourself to a spa day?"

Her lips parted in surprise over hearing Mark mention a spa day. "Do you even know what a spa day is?"

"Not fully. There's a day spa that just opened up on Pearl. Apparently, women like to go to it. It might be better to go on a weekday when it's less busy."

Mark pulled into a parking place near the café. He parked, turned off the ignition, and gave her an expectant look.

"Do you want me to take a spa day? If so, why?" Did he think that spa days were miraculous or something? Maybe he thought it was some type of feminine panacea that solved all problems.

His shoulders went up in a shrug. "You could if you wanted to. I thought maybe you could call in. You've told me enough times that you covered for fellow nurses who gave themselves the day off. Why not you?"

"I don't know. At first, I wanted to stop working to devote myself to the inn. While the inn still needs my devotion, it also needs my paycheck." Her lips pursed as her eyes rolled upward. "Things have been slow at work. Nothing like good weather to keep folks out of the hospital. Not as many illnesses floating around either. No one wants any surgery they can postpone until after vacation season. The post op floor has been a little slow. This is coming from the man who had to be shot to take a day off? I don't get it."

"Forensic anthropologist. I expect you want to be there when she nibs around your inn."

It made sense. Men thought women beat around the bush. The idea had promise though.

Donna's hand went up to rub her neck. "I feel a headache coming on. I better call now to give them time to get someone."

A feeling of excitement and dread gripped her as she pulled out her phone. The idea of calling the head nurse, who was also a friend, had her biting her lip. No way she could lie to her. Shelley would hear it in her voice. She pecked out a text saying she couldn't make it into work.

Shelley sent an immediate reply, proving she must have had the phone in front of her. Donna read it and laughed. "I was worried for nothing. Shelley says no worries. Light patient load. Have fun."

"There you go. You can now officially call yourself a rebel."

Not like that label would ever stick.

The new café was bright and cheery. A smiling hostess handed them menus with several small plates and homemade soups listed. There were so many she wanted to try. If a soup was extraordinary, she had no issues with buying it for the inn. She discovered after the first month the inn was open that she could not make every pastry, every cookie, every morsel of bread her clients consumed. She didn't have the time, and it turned out to be not as cost-effective as she assumed. Sometimes, the guests even preferred the bakery loaves she bought.

Halfway through her creamy wild mushroom soup and chicken kebobs with peanut sauce, her phone chimed. It would be nice to ignore it and enjoy the respite from all her pressing worries. Only she'd worry more about not answering it and who it could be.

"Hello?"

"She's here."

She recognized Tennyson's voice and was about ready to ask *who* was there. She assumed it was the forensic anthropologist, but you could never tell with her employee. Sometimes he made comments as if in the middle of an on-going conversation, thinking she automatically knew what he meant.

"The doctor and her mini-me and friend."

"Okay. We'll be there as soon as possible. Don't open the tarp until I'm there. Give her something to drink. Show them their rooms. Feed her."

"You want me to fix them something to eat?"

The shock in his voice almost made her laugh, but she knew Ten well enough to know his pretense at being clueless kept him from doing many tasks he didn't want to do. "Come on, you can put some sandwiches together. There are individual bags of chips in the pantry and fruit in the fridge. There's always the possibility that they might not be hungry, too. See you soon."

She hung up before Ten could protest his assignment. Mark put down his tea and picked up the rest of his bison burger. He waved it in her direction. "Do we get to finish lunch before we go charging out of here?"

"Yes. Ten is going to fix them lunch."

"Maria is there."

"She needs to handle incoming guests. Ten can do this."

Thankfully, Mark continued chewing and didn't mention anything about the boy's previous fails in the innkeeping trade. Sometimes, tough love was needed to motivate folks, or at least that was her theory. The rest of the meal wasn't nearly as enjoyable as she plowed through to get it done with. As they left, she snagged a to-go menu since the soup was memorable enough to have on hand. It didn't even come close to her chicken and dumpling soup, but it wouldn't take three hours to make either.

Convenience had become her byword as opposed to handcrafted, which was what was printed in their brochures. When you got right down to it, everything had to be handcrafted somewhere, even in a factory.

The drive back to the inn went fast as Donna constructed a mental image of a scholarly professor. When she wasn't doing that, she reassured herself that Ten could handle a quick lunch. If anything went wrong, Maria was on hand to put out the fire, not that there should be one with only cold cuts and chips.

As they pulled into the gravel parking lot, Donna spotted Ten talking to a pair of attractive women. He was grinning ear to ear and gesturing like crazy.

"Will you look at that?"

Mark gave a short nod. "I see. This bone recovery will be especially hard on our Tennyson."

Good heavens, it had all the makings of a soap opera with Ten already attached to Sloane, a local girl. "Just what we don't need."

"Please. Nothing will come of it. He'll tell his guy friends that the women were all over him, which would be a lie."

"Good to know. I wonder where the pathologist is?"

Chapter Seven

DONNA SWUNG OPEN her car door, not even waiting for Mark to do it for her. She was already striding toward the women by the time he'd rounded the car. As she drew closer, how young they were struck her. One couldn't be more than seventeen. She wore a T-shirt, that didn't quite do the job, showing a three-inch gap of tanned skin between it and her cutoffs. That couldn't be right, since they were supposedly college students. The other one had her hair pulled up into a ponytail. Her T-shirt actually reached her waistband. Now, she could accept her as a college student. She had a little more age and polish.

A man with a salt and pepper beard exited the back door. Who was that? She tried to catch Mark's eyes, but it was impossible since he had his head inside the trunk investigating the mysterious box. While she was used to guests roaming tame over the inn and its grounds, none exited via the back door, if she excluded the visit from eccentric amateur sleuth, Eunice.

The man made a beeline toward the women and held up a cell phone. "Dr. Haddox. Your cell was ringing."

The ponytailed woman took the phone.

"Thanks, Kelvin." She glanced down at the phone, frowned a little, then stuffed it in her back pocket. She turned toward Ten and asked, "When is your wacky employer going to be back, so we can get started?"

Tennyson saw Donna and gulped. *Yeah, when was the wacky employer arriving?* Of course, it didn't mean Ten had said that. More likely he'd call her *controlling*, not *wacky*. She narrowed her eyes at the woman in question. This kid was her forensic paleontologist. What could she know about the past? The female hadn't even experienced the blessed isolation of not having a cell phone and being connected twenty-four seven.

Mark slipped up behind her and whispered in her ear. "Everyone has to start somewhere."

"What do you mean?" His cryptic remarks used to irritate her until she discovered he was always more than willing to explain what he meant. It wasn't a game where she had to assemble the pieces on her own without any direction.

"You've already switched into battle mode. Your shoulders are back and fists clenched. Not sure why, but I assume you've decided the woman is useless because she's young."

"That's not true." Actually, it might be a little bit. Who calls someone wacky she'd never met? Add to that, Donna had to abandon her own bedroom at the inn and camp out at the paint fume house, formerly known as Mark's residence.

He nudged her, then gave her a kiss on the cheek. "You're so easy to read."

She didn't like that. How in the world would she win their bet about fooling him if he knew whatever she was thinking? "I just want the skeleton gone and the elevator guys back."

Mark kept his face close to her ear as he continued in a low voice. "We got Dr. Haddox almost overnight since she and her team want the experience."

"*Need* the experience is more like it."

"Are you determined to make this harder than it has to be?"

Her audible exhale announced at least some of her sentiments. She hated when he made a valid point. Although part of the time, if she were honest about it, she also relied on him doing so. "No."

"All she has to do is determine the age of the skeleton, which may or may not help us identify it. At least it will give us a direction for our search. Let's go meet the woman."

"Let's."

Mark led the way, and Donna reluctantly followed. It wasn't the first time someone had made an unpleasant remark about her. Although often the remarks made didn't necessarily upset her when what many thought were insults, she viewed as compliments. Other nurses complained she was a taskmaster, a rule follower, a workaholic. The last one wasn't entirely true, lately. If she was a workaholic, then she changed her focus from the hospital to the inn.

It might help if the woman wasn't so wrinkle-free and perfect. She could be on the cover of a fashion magazine wearing something a little more dramatic than a college T-shirt.

Mark introduced himself and her.

The woman held out her hand and smiled. "Pleased to meet you."

How had she missed the accent before? Her mind mentally replayed what she'd heard the woman say as she took the offered hand and clasped it. "Dr. Haddox, I presume?"

Instead of a traditional response, the paleontologist wrinkled her nose. "It's hard for me to get used to the name."

"Doctor?"

"No. Haddox. I decided to take my husband's name, but I still think of myself as Popov, which is a good Russian name that goes with a proud lineage."

The emphatic manner the words were delivered, Donna almost

expected some majestic Russian music to swell up in the background, along with a cast of at least a dozen Slavic models to step forward, looking off into the distance showing their noble profiles.

Being Russian explained the accent, which could mean she didn't say *wacky*. What could she have meant to say? Batty? Yaky? Neither was much better. "No matter what your name, I'm glad you came down to look at our skeleton."

Mark's eyes twinkled, probably amused by her effort to play nice. No matter, she'd get the job done. What she needed to do was get the woman started. "Tell me what you need?"

She gestured to the yard. "We can have the staging area here."

The younger girl dashed off in the direction of the van emblazoned with the college name. The bearded guy followed.

"Staging area?"

Instead of the doctor explaining, Ten attempted to. He mimicked her gesture, throwing his arm out to the hundred plus year old oak tree that shaded a good part of the yard. "Normally, they'd study the bones for clues as they were found, but since the elevators guys scrambled them around there's no point. They'll assemble the bones under the tree."

That made sense. *Yippee.* Her nose wrinkled as she pictured the group hovering over a blue tarp trying to complete a human skeleton jigsaw puzzle. Any outdoor activities she'd planned for her inn included lunch alfresco with floral tablecloths and lemonade chock full of ice and halved strawberries. There could be an occasional croquet game or people taking advantage of the rockers she'd put on the front porch. However, nowhere in her scenarios did a skeleton or a Russian paleontologist exist.

On the upside, it shouldn't last long. "How much time do you think it will take?"

Dr. Haddox shrugged her shoulders, as Tennyson rushed to explain. Somehow, he'd appointed himself as official liaison.

"Impossible to tell without the bones. Come back later for a more accurate guess."

Did he just tell her to come back later? Her eyebrows shot up as she growled low in her throat. "Did you hear what Ten just said to me?"

"Yep," Mark answered, but sensing her irritation, continued talking. "Don't embarrass him."

The idea that Mark thought she'd say something that would somehow shame Ten made her suck in her lips. So much for being the kinder, gentler version of herself. In the end, she defaulted to her normal operating mode. The fact her hubby said something to her chafed, but not as much as him being right. Thankfully, the clank and clatter of metal drew everyone's attention elsewhere.

The bearded guy and the girl returned with an aluminum table they unfolded and attempted to find level ground to set up. Tree roots buckled the soil making it hard to find a smooth spot, which was one of the reasons Donna had yet to serve lunch al fresco. That, along with the fact that most of her guests were not around for lunch. Then there was the neighbor issue. Anything that happened outside appeared to be an open invitation to the nearby gawkers and gossipers.

Dr. Haddox put her hands together in a prayer-like pose. "Ella and Kelvin have the table set up. We can start."

Yeah, start now, finish sooner. The mantra sounded in her head. Too bad the bone people couldn't hear it. If they could hear it, she'd add on to it. *Don't let it be anything that would cause further investigation and slow down my elevator.* Call her selfish. The elevator was to help her less mobile guests—so technically, it wouldn't be selfish.

Dr. Haddox, her assistants, and even Ten were staring at her. Had she said the words aloud? *Drats.* People always worked better when they thought it was their idea.

Mark nudged her shoulder. "They're waiting for you to do something. Maybe rip off the tarp or something."

"Oh." Thank goodness that was all. She carefully picked her way to the tarp-covered area and grabbed a handful of blue and pulled. *Nothing.* The plastic stayed in place. Not only did it not give, but she would have sworn it pulled back.

Mark joined her. "Let me try."

He gave the tarp a tug that yielded nothing. The color in his cheeks flared before he gave it another hefty pull. Finally, a few heavy-duty staples pulled free.

Donna reached for the loose tarp. "Here I was worried about the locals snooping. We can pull together and get it done."

The two of them had a sturdy grip on it and jerked backward hard in tandem. The heavy plastic that had been so resistant to opening gave suddenly, sending them both to the ground in a flurry of arms, legs, and muttered comments best not mentioned.

The blue tarp fluttered down covering them. The smell of moist air enveloped them along with a fine coating of concrete dust and earth. Muffled voices sounded outside the tarp.

"I can see the bones. Ella, go get my kit. Kelvin, I need the heavy-duty lights and flashlight."

Donna heard the feet rush off to do the doctor's bidding. Mark had already batted away his side of the tarp and pulled the blue plastic sheeting off Donna. He offered his hand to help her up, which she accepted. Normally, she would have refused, trying to prove to others she was capable of getting up on her own, but the way today was going, she accepted his hand.

As soon as she cleared the ground, Maria popped out of the house and waved frantically at her. Oh goodie, another crisis. She cut her eyes toward Mark and announced, "I'll be right back."

He grinned at her assertion, then gestured to the trio, now peering into the hole with Ten lingering nearby as if he might be asked to assist. "I can handle this."

"I know you can." The man could stand around all day and ride herd on the crew, but unfortunately, he would have to take his shift at the convention center or whatever petty duty the chief had assigned him. Gen Con Snag, as the local merchants called it, was the coup of the century. The insidious bed bugs nixed the previous city, and Legacy got it only because they underbid everyone else. She wasn't entirely sure, but the new convention center may have been free or close to it since the new owner wanted to get the word out of its existence. The Con served as a proving ground to see if Legacy could successfully handle so many tourists at once.

One part of the equation was the police. Mainly, their job would be to keep the traffic flowing. All it took was one or two non-locals turning up a one-way street, causing a snarl in the afternoon traffic. Most of the one-way streets weren't marked since everyone knew which streets were which, the lack of signs serving as a rite of passage for new drivers. Donna even had her own story of driving her tiny compact car on the sidewalk when she was sixteen. With any luck, they got all the new streets signs up on time.

Bed bugs. The very idea made a full body shiver go through her as she pondered the insect. They had plenty of insects this far south, some of them quite large. The bed bug hadn't been an issue like it had been in the bigger cities such as New York and Los Angeles. Those places had tons of hotels and people, which equated to breeding grounds for the louse that loved to nibble on a resting human.

Her research revealed that the bugs traveled via human hosts, often hitching rides on luggage, purses, even clothes. There had to be a way to ensure the insects didn't make a stop at her place. The prevention article included several tips, including caulking any easy entry points. Another reason to get the elevator finished, especially considering her last unwelcome guest was a raccoon. The article went on to mention washing and drying clothes in high heat, quarantining purses, bagging luggage in oversize garbage bags, and keeping everything ruthlessly clean. The cleaning she didn't have any issue with. Maybe she could offer a free laundry service for the guests, which would be even more work. Still, if it kept her bed bug-free, she'd do it.

The prospect of how to prevent bed bugs consumed her as she entered the inn. Inside, Maria waited in the kitchen. The calm demeanor she normally exhibited was missing. Her top teeth worried her bottom lip while she turned her wedding ring on her finger.

"Thank goodness you got here."

Donna inhaled, prepping herself for whatever the issue was. In her daydreams, running a bed and breakfast had been a relaxing experience. She soon discovered only the guests were able to kick back. "What's up?"

"I booked all the guests like I normally do."

"That you do." So far, she didn't see a problem.

"Each room is listed as one or two beds."

"True."

"I naturally assumed if a person booked a one-bed room that both people would sleep in the same bed."

"Natural assumption." She could see where this was going. "They need another bed?"

"Exactly."

Not like she had to worry about competition since there were no beds to be had. "Tell them the city is booked, but we can provide a rollaway bed, free of charge."

"That might work, but we don't have a rollaway bed."

"We will in a little bit. I'll order one. Daniel can pick it up on his lunch break and deliver it. I'm much too busy to do it."

Maria was halfway to the interior door now that she had a solution to her dilemma. "You might want to restock the pantry on the second floor. I've already had someone ask me for more delicious butter cookies. The fact we're allowing early check-ins makes us popular, but I think most of the guests rushed here and haven't had lunch. Oh, I forgot to mention one of our guests is a merchant at the convention."

"So? Why should that matter?"

"He wanted to know where to park his trailer."

"There's no way he can park his trailer in our tiny parking lot and not block everyone."

"That's what I thought, too. I told him to park in front."

Donna closed her eyes. Here she thought the public assembling of the skeleton was going to upset her snooty neighbors, although she'd point out she couldn't be held responsible for what happened at the inn before she owned it. The inn had been vacant for several years and before that, it served as a VFW post with only street parking. Before Donna could answer Maria had already left.

A baby coo had her glancing toward the playpen. Baby Cici kicked her chubby legs in the air and smiled. Baby experts declare babies don't smile immediately, but merely imitate their parents' facial expressions until six months or older. Maybe Cici was more advanced than most. She was smiling, and Donna would bet good money the child was not imitating her at this point in time. If she were, she'd have pulled her hair up into clumps and have stress lines on her forehead.

Donna scooped up her niece and snuggled her on her shoulder. Nothing like the smell of fresh baby complete with powder, except her niece was a little less than sweet smelling. Another sniff indicated that Cici needed to be changed. Yeah, just her luck. After changing her and putting her in another outfit Donna found in the bag, she carried Cici and the plastic bag wrapped offensive diaper outside. Her plan was to get rid of the diaper outside since she didn't want that foul odor in her inn.

On her way to the trashcan, she couldn't help noticing a small crowd gathered around the table. The doctor and her assistants were a given. Mark and Tennyson were no surprise, but the dogwalker duo and their standard poodle had joined the group. Jasper, her dog, would not like this one bit. Her lips pursed since she was not overly pleased with the development, either.

Donna inched closer to see what was happening. A clavicle bone rested on the table and Dr. Haddox pointed to it as she spoke. "We're fortunate to recover the clavicle first. It's usually the last to stop growing. This happens at the age of twenty in women and earlier in men."

Why did everything she say in her accented English sound so exotic? The woman could probably sell retread tires with that accent.

One of the dog walkers interrupted her explanation with a query. "You're not going to use carbon dating?"

Dr. Haddox gave an exquisite, tinkling laugh. Somehow, Donna suspected she'd have an adorable laugh. Instead of scolding the man, the paleontologist beamed at him as she replied.

"Carbon dating is for bones much older. At least 5000 years or more. We can see by the color and density of the bones, even the size, they are at most a hundred years old."

Please be a hundred years old, so no criminal procedures will be needed. The entire premise behind a hundred years statute of limitations was that any murderer who had committed the crime would be dead, leaving no need to pursue criminal proceedings.

"Do you know how old the person was?" Tennyson asked the question Donna wanted to ask.

The doctor gave him an approving nod before answering. "With one bone, I cannot even tell you the gender. I will need the pelvic girdle to do so. The skull with the teeth will allow me to get a time window based on dental work. Sometimes, it hints at ethnic origin since different countries have different dental procedures. I appreciate your interest, but I must work." She sniffed the air twice with her aristocratic nostrils flaring, then made a moue of distaste. "What is that smell?"

Yeah, what was that horrible smell? Little Cici was snuggled into her left side and was contently playing with the ends of Donna's hair. However, the dirty diaper was still gripped in her right hand. She slipped away without a word. Probably just as well, no reason to be exposing her niece to a possible murder no matter how long ago it happened. Although, if the child stuck around the inn long, the possibilities of one happening in the future were unfortunately high.

Chapter Eight

B Y ONE PM, all of the guests had taken advantage of the early check-in. A few dumped their luggage, took the printed schedule Maria handed them, and commented where they would go first. The smart vendors had arrived a day early and already had their merchandise displayed at the Center.

A younger couple wearing graphic art T-shirts chattered as they strolled down the foyer.

"We really need to get to the Center and sign up for the tournaments and LARP adventures."

The other partner stumbled to a stop and gave the woman a disbelieving stare. "You didn't sign up online? I always sign up online. You get the best spots that way."

The woman grimaced. "Sometimes you cut yourself out of panels and workshops or anything they added at the last minute by signing up online."

The conversation amused Donna with trying to decide if she and Mark were attending Gen Con as opposed to working it, which part of the couple would they be? She'd probably be the planner who wanted to assure they got prime spots but would include some space for the spontaneous. Wonder what Mark would be? Better yet, where was the man?

The tempting smell of barbeque invited her outside. Her sweetie was manning the grill. She thought it might be a perk to provide some handheld food for the guests. She assumed they were not the wine and appetizers crowd. Besides, there were probably too many things they wanted to do tonight as opposed to mingling with the other guests and talking in low voices about the weather and travel conditions. Her real reason behind providing free food was to keep her bone folks fed. If they stopped to eat and tried their luck at the town's packed eateries, it would only delay moving the skeleton on to its appropriate home.

Whose skeleton was it anyway? It could easily be a former owner or relative interred into the soil before the house was ever built. That would be an acceptable possibility. So much better than someone being killed at the inn, then hidden in the cellar. She'd never been a fan of a dirt cellar, but even less so now, considering there might be even more bones just waiting to be discovered. The prospect made her shiver.

Mark held court at the gas grill. A few purists would complain, stating authentic barbeque required wood briquets. It wasn't an argument she cared to be a part of any more than she wanted to swelter in the summer heat cooking meat that could easily be prepared in the oven. The smell of slightly charred food worked as a siren song, drawing in other men who would arrange themselves around the grill and reminisce about the meat they'd cooked. If any of the neighborhood men were to stop by in hopes of a good story or a brew, they would be disappointed if they found Donna flipping burgers. There was an unwritten rule that all food made outside had to be done by a male. It must go back to their hunter heritage, although some would have to go way back to find an ancestor capable of running down dinner.

Masculine laughter erupted as she walked down the steps. A few of the neighborhood men were gathered on the concrete slab located between her parking lot and garage. She wasn't sure what the VFW had used the slab for, but it did make a nice grill spot. An umbrella shaded the table where the utensils and spices rested along with the towel covered meat. A few of the neighbors sat in iron wrought chairs while another stood close to Mark, conversing.

Didn't anyone have a real job around here?

The visible wrinkles and silver hair indicated that the seated men were retirement age or close to it. The tall, dark-haired man was some sort of investment counselor, who wrote books on the same subject. When he wasn't trying to wrestle 401K retirement plans away from their original investment companies to his, he touted his books, even going so far as to bring one to the inn's open house. Barry never actually gave them his book, just showed it off, mentioning several times he would be available for signing if someone purchased it at any of the local retailers.

By the time she reached the group they were in an animated discussion. Forcing a smile, she nodded to the men. She'd seen all of them in the neighborhood, but she only knew Barry by name.

One of the silver-haired gents worked himself to the edge of his chair asking, "So, Mark, what's your take on this skeleton business?"

Her husband, spotting her, smiled but turned to answer the query. "Family graveyard. I assume the house was built over it."

Good gracious. He was repeating the story she'd told Ten. Plenty of English mysteries featured skeletons discovered in the cellars of old homes. Since the older homes had dirt floor cellars, it was always easy enough to inter a family member or even a stranger for that matter.

The man who'd asked the question made a derisive snort at Mark's reply. "Come on. You can do better than that. If you really thought that, why would you have the CSI crew over there?" He gestured to the squad separating concrete rubble and bones from the dirt using screen boxes.

This is how rumors started. Ignorant people making assumptions. Before Mark could answer, she did.

"Dr. Haddox is not part of a crime scene investigation."

The doctor must have heard her name because she waved at them. She said something to the assistants who headed toward the house as she strolled toward the barbeque club. The men immediately smiled at the sight of the pretty blonde.

"Gentleman," she addressed the group, leaving Donna out of her greeting. "I'm Dr. Kim Haddox, a full professor of forensic science at Western Carolina University. I am also a licensed paleontologist, specializing in human bones."

The neighbors acted suitably impressed, but Donna guessed they didn't hear a word the woman said, being too interested in cataloging her charms. Mark's amused gaze caught hers. They both acknowledged the doctor's use of her full job title with just a slight nod. It was great being able to talk without saying a word. The woman may have resorted to her job title to prove she was more than just a pretty face.

Dr. Haddox continued to explain in detail what she was doing and what she could determine by analyzing the bones. One of the older gentlemen caught the eye of another man and mouthed the word, *spy*. It wasn't real hard to lipread that one word. The Russian accent must have caused that assumption. She did not need people thinking she had a spy at her inn, but then, it was better than a dead body.

Mark made a gesture to her about a drink. Yeah, she should have brought him something, considering the man was probably dehydrated. Since everyone would appreciate a drink, she pivoted and made her way to the house. If she hurried, she would be back before Dr. Haddox finished her lecture on the nature of bones and their use in forensic science.

Fortunately, she had a readymade pitcher of lemonade in the fridge. She poured the liquid into glasses of ice and decided at the last minute on a plate of cookies. Some hostesses would have left the pitcher outside, but that would give her no excuse to return and check on everyone. A person shouldn't have to manufacture a reason to ramble about on her own property, but she resorted to one anyhow. South Carolina might have officially been voted the politest state, but North Carolina wasn't far behind.

She hefted up the heavy tray, wondering for a moment where Ten was. He could have delivered it for her. Although, if he did, she wouldn't be able to gather the gossipy tidbits. She could ask Mark, but for such an observant man he could be maddeningly vague about some things. He might even mention they talked about *stuff*. Maybe that was a cover for guy talk, which usually included football, barbeque techniques, and broads.

Her biceps strained as she carried the heavy tray, while a few of the chattering guests weaved past her, deep in discussion about an upcoming tournament. Her eyes stayed on the two young men and slender female. In her day, a person would offer help. As if hearing her thoughts, one of the males glanced back, then turned around.

"Can I carry that for you?"

Was the sky blue? "Yes, you can."

She waited until her unknown helper had a firm grip on the tray before letting go. She gestured to where the grill team was seated. "Over there on the table."

"Sure." He delivered the tray, waved at the chatty gentlemen and then sprinted after his friends.

It made her appearance a little out of place since she hadn't arrived with the refreshments. It took a bit of a skip and a jog to get there before the men helped themselves, negating her purpose, but she made it.

"Nice of him to help." She wasn't sure of how to segue into the conversation. Most of the men hanging out didn't know as much as her former neighbor Herman. None of them had lived in the neighborhood long enough to have any history of the area. Her neighbors acted like they were some type of Legacy aristocracy, which was a laugh considering the town founders left about the same time the textile mills did.

The gentlemen smiled at her arrival, but Donna couldn't help but notice the smiles weren't as bright as what they'd given the Russian paleontologist.

Oh well, it was better that way. People tended to relax when they were around people they neither feared nor felt the need to impress. Apparently, she fit the bill. In the beginning, the neighbors made an effort to discourage her from turning the decaying Victorian into an inn. Now, they grudgingly tolerated her, some more than others. The majority always made an appearance at her open houses and gobbled as many goodies as they could before retreating to their own homes.

Each frosty glass of lemonade was welcomed with an appreciative murmur. She carried Mark's to him. Grilling in the summer heat was not for the faint of heart. It had to be close to two. Donna checked her watch just to be sure.

"Don't worry," Mark spoke in a low voice for her ears alone. "My shift doesn't start until six."

Six pm! Her eyebrows shot up. Putting a thirty-year veteran on such an undesirable shift was nothing less than a slap in the face, but it would prime the rumor mill if she ranted about Billings within their hearing. Even if they had similar feelings, they still would spread it far and wide. She handed Mark his glass, then closed her eyes and took a deep breath. Finally, she allowed herself to speak.

"I think it would be better if I go back to the house. I, ah, have some errands to do."

Mark recognized her internal struggle to act like nothing was wrong. "That might be best. I'll bring the meat in when it's done."

She walked slowly back to the house, hoping to regain some of her earlier calm. In the midst of wanting to corner Billings and give him a piece of her mind, she realized something. Her hubby was employing a tried and true method of gathering masculine gossip. It would be good to know what he found out, but for now, she'd concentrate on her live guests. If she had time, she'd do an online search for Joseph Carpenter.

An odd tune ripped through the air. It had the tinny quality more associated with horns than radios. It sounded again, closer, forcing Donna to change her direction and head to the front of the inn where a giant wiener car was parallel parking. *Mercy! What next?* Her one hand lost its grip on the empty tray allowing it to bang against her leg.

The front door opened as Maria stepped out and waved in the direction of the truck. She apparently didn't spot Donna as she came down the stairs. She continued to wave at whoever was driving the monstrosity. Finally, she cupped her hands around her mouth and yelled.

"You need to park farther up! You're blocking the inn sign."

Donna hadn't even considered that possibility, too overwhelmed with the sight of the giant hot dog van. Maybe this was some huge prank. If so, whoever planned it could have picked a better time. A man climbed out of the van showing he either hadn't heard Maria's request or didn't care.

The ponytailed male circled his vehicle and walked toward the inn. He was hard to miss with his bright yellow shirt emblazoned with a happy hot dog. One could only assume the meat sausage was delighted at the possibility of being cooked and eaten.

When he reached Maria, he grabbed and hugged her, which resulted in Jasper charging out of the bushes and barking. The man released her fast. Donna wasn't sure if it was due to the canine security system or Maria stomping on the man's instep. It was probably the latter.

"Come on, sister! I thought you southerners were more welcoming than that."

Donna decided to intervene before another guest ended up dead. "Hello there. Donna Tollhouse—Taber." She hadn't totally decided on what name to use after her marriage. "I own the inn."

The man glanced in her direction. "I suppose you want a hug, too."

"No." He didn't have to look so put out about the idea. Personally, she could pass on anything the man was giving out, but she did hope his credit was good. "None of the employees at the inn would appreciate any physical contact. At this inn, we use our words."

Now she sounded like she was teaching preschool, but it did appear the man had missed the lesson about keeping your hands to yourself. "How can I help you?"

"Jason Mulder. I'm checking in. I need to get a key for my room, then I'm off to the convention center."

Since he arrived in the hot dog van, then he'd take it with him. "I assume" she pointed to the vehicle, "you'll be driving that."

"You go to the head of the class."

Donna glanced at her watch out of curiosity. It had hardly been five minutes, and the man had already stretched her patience to its limit. Maria backed up slowly and darted inside the building. Donna wouldn't be surprised if her sister-in-law barred the door. A few seconds later, Maria came back with a room key and handed it to Jason 'Annoying' Muldur.

"You're on the third floor, second door. They're all numbered. Match the key number up to the door number, and you'll be fine."

The patronizing tone of voice Maria employed was foreign to Donna. She'd never heard it before. Apparently, it had no impact on Jason. There was a long honk as Daniel pulled in behind the wiener mobile. He yelled as soon as he exited his truck.

"How's my beautiful wife today?"

Jason glanced back in Daniel's direction and took a definite step back.

Really? Two women and a dog made it clear that Jason's overtures were unwelcome and he's the one that acts offended, but when a man shows up, it's a different story?

Someone must have turned on the flashing sign that notified the menfolk that help is needed. Mark rounded the house carrying a spatula and still in his barbeque apron that announced *This cook is red hot!*

"What's going on here?" He used his gravelly *I mean business* tone.

Hot dog guy shrugged his shoulders as if he had no clue. Emboldened by the show of familiar faces, Jasper stepped closer to the offender and growled. "Call off your dog. All I need is a place to sleep. If this is the way you welcome outsiders this might be your last Gen Con."

His words, instead of creating fear and trembling as he might have expected, had Donna and Mark exchanging pleased looks. The convention hadn't even started, and she was already tired of it. Girls weekends or even the slightly out of control Columbus Days seemed preferable, but maybe she was basing it on one obnoxious vendor, a dead guest, a skeleton, and a micromanaging police commissioner.

Chapter Nine

O<small>NLY A FEW</small> bread crumbs remained on the platter, along with an errant ketchup squirt. Donna picked up the empty platter and carried it to the kitchen. When she'd placed the full platter on the dining room server, she would have sworn most of her guests had left until they swarmed the table, carrying off cans of soda and individual chip bags, along with the burgers. Only one male guest with slipping glasses thanked her. At least his mother had brought him up right.

She tried to remember his face, or anything that made her polite guest memorable, to be able to mention him to Maria who might be able to identify him. Her brow furrowed as she tried to remember. The chaos that ensued after she encouraged a passing guest to make free with food she'd set on the server wiped out everything else. Before she even put the buns on the rest of the burgers, she made sure Ten carried out a tray to the forensic team. No reason for them to stop work or clean up. The nurse in her sent out a bottle of hand disinfectant and a roll of paper towels. Dr. Haddox's group stopped for an early dinner but thankfully returned to work since the summer light would be strong enough until six.

She placed the platter in the dishwasher before reaching for a rag. In the dining room, she pushed in some chairs and then wiped down the server. Her gaze went to the empty buffet as she wiped off the condensation left by the refrigerated drinks. The empty box that had held the chip bags she stuck under her arm. It was as if a swarm of locusts had descended and taken everything edible. There couldn't be more than sixteen people at the most staying at the inn. It certainly felt like more had swooped in and carried off the food. She'd even flattened herself against the wall as a trio sprinted to the table as if the food would vanish as suddenly as it appeared.

Ten wandered into the dining room with a forlorn expression. "It looks like they ate everything. The pigs."

His outrage made her chuckle since he could be quite the eater, too. "No worries. I hid some burgers for you."

"Yes!" He gave a short fist pump. "Where?"

"Microwave. They may still be warm. Go check." Donna followed him into the kitchen. "One of those burgers is mine. I had no clue they'd be gobbled up like that. I think I had twenty on that platter, and they were the quarter pounder ones."

Her employee already had the plate in his hand and carried it to the kitchen island. Donna reached for a burger just in case Tennyson hadn't heard her. It wasn't hot anymore, but she was past caring. A low growl indicated her stomach's feeling on the matter. The condiments were still in the dining room. Instead of placing the burger back on the plate and chance Ten accidentally consuming it, she carried it with her.

Cradling the ketchup and mustard in the crook of her elbow while holding the pickle jar by the lid, she backed into the kitchen. The glass jar crashed to the floor sending pickles, pickle juice, and shards of glass exploding across the room. Jasper, jolted from sleep, erupted into a barking frenzy.

"Crud!" Her fingers were still curled around the metal lid of the jar. "I knew better than to carry the jar by its lid. Obviously, the ravagers didn't bother to tighten it."

Jasper growled at the offending pickle slices, darting in to nip at one. Ten herded the dog out of the room.

Great. She'd have to clean it up and forgo a pickle on her burger, and she did love her pickles, especially the classic dill. She placed the other condiments on the island along with the useless lid. A little water would net her a couple of pickles. She peered at the green globs on the floor, squinting to see if any of them were glass free. The last thing she needed was a shard of glass in her intestine.

The sound of the mop bucket on wheels signaled Ten's return. He entered, talking, "You'd think the guests hadn't eaten in a year, and I saw some of them carry those ol' camp coolers in. The types you see sometimes in the back of trucks."

Donna groaned, thinking about wet spots on her hardwood floors. "Here, let me sweep as much glass and pickles as I can."

She picked up big chunks of the jar and threw them into the trash as Ten commented on their visitors. "I get the cooler. It's expensive to eat out every meal. At least they get breakfast here."

Donna had swept the majority of pickles into the dustpan only half-listening to Ten when his words registered. She straightened up and knocked the pickles into the trash. "What guest?"

Ten shrugged his shoulders. "Dunno. Why does it matter?"

"I guess it doesn't. Just curious." Nothing she could put her finger on besides an obsessive need to know the details. "If I had some jumbo cooler I wanted to sneak past the innkeeper, I'd use the elevator, too."

"Is there a rule against coolers?"

"No." She straightened and gestured to the floor, signaling it was Ten's turn to take over with the mop. The broom and dustpan ended up on the back porch where she could spray them off.

Donna stood there looking at the forensic workers huddled over the table, but not really seeing them. Her mind was on coolers. The Painted Lady Inn was not some motor lodge that road crews used. It was a high-class establishment with charm and atmosphere. B and Bs did provide a place to lay your head, but they were supposed to bring in more revenue to the area. Her guests should be dining at the local eateries, although she hadn't helped with that by providing burgers. Hopefully, there would be no need to cook anything else for the forensic team.

The angle of the sun had made a hard drop westward. People used to living on the east coast expected a sunset that went on forever, dipping behind mountains, but still sending up rays of light. Not so on the North Carolina coast where the sun made the gradual slide across the sky, then dropped out of sight, which was something the lifeguards tried to warn the tourists about. The beach had no lights. The unexpected darkness had tourists stumbling toward the bordering homes and restaurants that threw out enough light to guide them back to shore. The real issue was the riptide that usually occurred at dusk and dawn often carrying an unwary swimmer away from the shoreline.

Maybe she should warn the team that night wasn't that far away. Before she made it all the way down the steps, Dr. Haddox approached her.

"We need to bring the skeleton inside."

"Inside?" She found herself parroting the word. "Why?"

"We don't want anything to happen to him." Dr. Haddox gave a shrug. "You know the town is full of strangers. It is hard to know what they might do."

The women had a point. Even without a town full of strangers, Donna didn't trust a few in her neighborhood not to pop over for a look-see and a souvenir. She could hear Tennyson yelling something, but she could only handle one thing at a time. His crisis could consist of something minor such as being out of root beer, which did happen on occasion.

"Okay. I assume you'll bag the bones and take them to your room?"

The woman held up one finger. "We need to continue working somewhere with room and a lot of light."

She couldn't mean to conduct a real-life Operation game in her kitchen. *Nope.* It wasn't going to happen. "There's no way you can use my kitchen. The board of health would not approve." They wouldn't approve of the dining room, either. That depended on the board of health showing up while they were assembling the skeleton, which she knew wouldn't happen since they had already been inspected in April.

"The dining room would work."

Her reluctance must have shown. Dr. Haddox tacked on, in her Russian accented English, "You told me to be fast. I am being fast, but now—you."

"Okay." She put her hands up as if surrendering. "Dining room table it is. I want to put plastic over it first."

"Of course."

"Sun's going down." Donna always hated when her brother stated the obvious and here she was doing it.

"I know. That's why we need to move the skeleton and the reason I asked."

Donna held her hand up to stop a repeat of her previous conversation. "Got it. Going to cover the tables now." She intended to eat her burger first. No need to mention that. She'd get the tables covered in plenty of time.

Her rubber-soled shoes slipped a little as she entered the kitchen.

Her hand found purchase on the island before she met the floor close up.

Tennyson, witnessing her almost fall, added belatedly, "The floor's wet."

"I noticed."

Jasper stood closer to the island, wolfing something down. Even though her elderly puggle was an only dog, he tended to gulp down his food as if a certain someone or something would pull it out of his mouth. Donna was about to ask what her pup was eating when she noticed an empty spot where she'd left her burger.

Good gravy! The burger was the only thing that was stopping her insides from munching on each other. "Tennyson! You didn't feed that dog my dinner, did you?"

The employee jerked as if hit, then slowly swiveled his bar stool to face her. "I did ask you. Didn't you hear me yelling?"

She *had* heard something while she'd been talking to Russian Barbie but couldn't decipher anything. "Did you hear me reply?"

"Um, no." His eyebrows lifted a little as his face reddened. "I figured since you didn't say anything it didn't matter, and Jasper looked so pitiful."

"Why didn't you give him one of your burgers? You had two." Why was it people were always free with other's people's stuff?

"Ate them." He shrugged his shoulders. "Yours was the only one left. Anyone would have thought you didn't want it since you left it. It was an honest mistake."

She'd returned from leaving the pickle-soaked broom and dustpan on the porch. It wasn't like she'd been away on a European tour. Instead of belaboring the point, she opened the refrigerator to search for something edible.

A half container of coleslaw that had already grown strong

squatted beside a variety of condiments. The lunchmeat drawer was empty, but there was a couple of gouda and cheddar cheese slices left. It looked like a grilled cheese sandwich and an evening run to the grocery were in her immediate future.

As she worked on her supper, Tennyson slunk out of the kitchen, pulling the mop bucket behind him. His behavior made her feel like she'd just sucked out the joy from the room. "Come back here, now."

He pointed to himself as if he had his doubts who she meant. After all, she could have meant Jasper, who had had enough sense to leave, too. "Yes, I mean you."

"I told you I was sorry."

"No, you told me it was a mistake." Before he could attempt an apology, she gestured with her spatula. "I didn't ask you to come back so you could apologize. I figured we could keep each other company while I ate my grilled cheese. Should I assume you'd like one, too?"

His avid expression told the tale along with his head bob.

"Good. I have enough cheese for two, but not anymore. I have to order groceries tonight."

Tennyson arched his eyebrow, hearing the unspoken request. "I'll pick them up."

"Great." At least that was one issue resolved. Of course, she needed to order the groceries, something she should have done yesterday, but a few major crises shoved that out of the way. The sound of footsteps on the back stoop had her dashing for the dining room and plastic tablecloths. She had bought a few at the dollar store printed with beach umbrellas and sand pails. Her original intention had been to make beach picnic baskets with them. So far, no one had ever asked for a picnic lunch.

She snapped a tablecloth in the air shaking out the wrinkles before smoothing it over the round table. No way a full-size skeleton could fit on a table less than forty inches across. Good heavens, that meant they'd use the full-size dining table she had pushed against the wall. Normally, people were not fans of sitting beside those they didn't know. The big table only came out for family dinners and receptions. She had no super-sized plastic tablecloth. "Ten!"

Her employee strolled out and glanced at the tables. "Breakfast is a long way off."

"I know that. Do we have any more tarps?"

He cocked his head back as if examining the ceiling, then shook his head. "We used them to cover the holes."

Daggummit! It was exactly as she thought. "I'll need the old sheets then. The ones that I told you to burn."

"How did you know I didn't burn them?"

Donna was unwilling to tell him that she saw them on his dresser when she peeked into his room in search of Jasper. It would make her appear nosy. "Burning ordinance. You know we can't burn anything in Legacy."

That appeared to be enough of an explanation. Tennyson vanished and returned in a matter of seconds with the sheets. Together, they covered the table just as the bone crew entered. Kelvin glanced around and made a disappointed whimper.

Jasper made the same sound when she failed to give him a treat. No doubt the man was looking for food, and there wouldn't be any until she got groceries. There were still a few things in the inn freezer.

"Over here." Donna gestured to the table they just finished covering. "I can rustle up some coffee and snacks if you want some."

The general murmur of approval settled the matter. Little did they know that snacks would consist of popcorn mixture with pretzels, peanuts, and breakfast cereal. If there was a bag of candy covered chocolate with a little *M* printed on them, she'd throw that in, too.

Once she had coffee started and the snack mix out, it was time to order her groceries. If she didn't hurry there wouldn't be time for Ten to pick them up, which would mean she'd have to go to the store herself. *Horror.* She gave an all over shiver. Normally, she didn't mind the grocery, especially if it was free sample day, but it took time she didn't have.

Tennyson wandered in as she booted the computer up. "How long before I need to pick the groceries up?"

"It would help if I ordered them first." She grimaced, then typed in the grocery name as soon as the Internet connection bars came up. "The store will tell me when it can get the order together. You better hope it's tonight, or you'll be pushing a grocery buggy around checking stuff off the list."

"Not that." He groaned and managed a pained expression.

No way she trusted him with the grocery selection. At least an anonymous employee whose job depended on keeping the customer happy might try a little harder. So far, she had no complaints about the pickup service, except that it didn't include delivery. A standing grocery list showed up that Donna approved. She added on some more snack foods and drinks. "Game playing must really work up an appetite."

"Dunno. Could, I guess." Tennyson hooked his foot on the bar stool rung and pulled it closer and took a seat. "Not sure if any of them have even played games. Most have just got here."

He had a point. "So, you met some of our guests? Any impressions?"

His hand rubbed his chin, making her grin at his mimicry of Mark's trademark gesture. Next, he'd clear his throat before making a comment. He coughed, then held up a finger as if to speak. *Nailed it.*

"Most are single and young."

"Yeah, that sounds about right."

"There were a few bearded dudes who could be old, like thirty or something."

Donna narrowed her eyes to bring into focus the times Ten could pick up her groceries. By the time he came back, she unpacked them, and set up the kitchen for breakfast, Mark might beat her back to the house. Her lips pursed as she considered the possibility as a good thing. The prospect of traipsing through a dark, empty house full of scaffolding and ladders didn't appeal. Remembering the conversation, she realized nothing had been said for a while. "They'd be willing to drive to some out of the way place. Once you settle down those days are behind you. Too immerse in doing family things and work-related functions. Did anyone stand out from the others?"

She was hoping he caught the name of the only guest who thanked her for her impromptu meal. It would be nice to have a name to go with the face.

"Yeah, there was one. A red-headed babe named Sasha." He grinned, then made a little sigh.

Donna reached across the island and poked him. "That was for your girlfriend you temporarily forgot about."

"Hey!" He brushed her hand away. "I remember Sloane. There's no rule against a man looking."

"There may not be a rule, but don't come crying to me when Sloane dumps you." She made a final click to submit her order.

"Pickup is at ten. You better head out at nine-thirty to be on time.

"That's late." He shot an accusing glance her way as if she made the time late on purpose.

"Please. I've seen you go out later to meet up with friends or go to a movie."

"That's different when it's social."

"That makes a difference, how?"

He shrugged his shoulder. "Just does. Did you make us any popcorn mix?"

By *us* he meant him. "Get a bowl and get some from the dining room. Then you can tell me what they're talking about."

Tennyson slipped from the stool and headed for the cabinet. "What are you going to be doing in here?"

"I'll be looking up information on our recently departed guest, Joseph Carpenter." There was no reason not to mention it, considering she made no mention of her belief that he may have been helped along his odd trip down the stairs. She hadn't pinpointed anything, yet. It was all a vague feeling. Donna kept it to herself due to that micromanaging nincompoop at the station who'd harass Mark if he caught wind of her suspicions. It would be better to gather all the information first.

"Oh, him." Tennyson grabbed a bowl and head for the door. "I know all about him. Sasha told me."

Chapter Ten

W HO WAS SASHA? The cute female part Tennyson thoroughly conveyed. Donna assumed she must be part of the Gen Con fans that descended upon Legacy. Why not corner her for a personal chat?

Yeah, that would go over well. A review would show up on Yelp with the title *Beware the Innkeeper.* A casual conversation like Tennyson had would be for the best. Now if only her employee paid attention as opposed to comparing Sasha with his current girlfriend in his mind. New usually won over the known, even when unknown could actually be worse. That would also explain the couples who married, divorced and then married each other again.

The best she could do was wait for Tennyson or look up the fellow on her own. After all, the computer was already up. Her first attempt at Joseph Carpenter brought her too many names. It made her wonder if his body had been picked up yet.

A quick call to her sweetie wouldn't be too out of place. Pulling her phone out of her pocket, she glanced toward the door. No sign of Tennyson, but she could hear him talking. It could be information gathering, which was a more pleasant thought than wasting time. Her thumb depressed the two. She'd had Mark's cell number programmed into her phone ever since she met him years ago over their first dead body.

As their relationship progressed, he moved up the speed dial list, nosing out Daniel and Mother for the coveted second position. One was always voice mail. The phone burbled in her ear, then was answered by a breathless Mark. "What's wrong?"

"Nothing. Does there have to be something wrong for me to call my loving husband?"

"You usually only call if something has spiraled out of control, and you need help, or you're nosing around for information."

"Goodness, that isn't too flattering!" It sounded a bit like her, but it didn't mean she had to like it.

"Why did you call, then?"

"Just wondering how your night was going?"

"Boring. Standing around the convention center, people watching."

"See anything interesting?"

"Not really. One of the attendees has a service potbellied pig instead of a dog, which is different."

"Lots of standing around and directing people to the bathroom?"

"Basically. So, that's why you called?"

Donna was ready to clarify her purpose when she could hear another voice through Mark's phone. It was at a distance, but she could still make out the words.

"That better be an official call."

No need for her to see the commissioner. She recognized that lack of personality anywhere. Wasn't it enough that he'd put a thirty-year veteran on what was basically a rookie assignment? Now he was monitoring phone calls? It would be no time before he had officers clocking in and out to go to the bathroom. She quietly hung up not wanting to hear anything else the man had to say. Her blood pressure was already high enough.

Her phone rang again before she could even put it in her pocket. Mark would want to know why she hung up like that.

She swiped to the right to answer, not even bothering to look at the number. "I had to hang up. I couldn't listen to that jerk anymore."

"Jerk? Who are you calling a jerk?"

The voice, while familiar, wasn't Mark's. It took her a second to recognize the jovial tone. "Herman!"

"That's me. You better not be calling me a jerk, especially before you even know why I called."

"No. Not you. Some things have changed around here." While she wanted to vent about the brain-dead commissioner, she knew her hubby wouldn't appreciate it. Her former neighbor might be a couple of states away, but it would be best not to take chances. He could have called someone else as easily as he called her and let slip just how she felt about the newest member of the Legacy Police Force.

A hoarse chuckle came over the line. "Yeah, I heard about it."

"You did?" Her brows beetled together as she tried to determine what he had heard, and better yet, from whom he had heard it.

"It's about time, too. I was beginning to think I'd never be around to see it happen. Thank goodness I managed to hang on long enough to finally see the mystery solved."

That knocked out the commissioner. Even though Donna had spent most of her life in Legacy, Herman had lived there much longer. The only mystery Herman had harped on over the years was the missing diamonds and a dead diamond thief found not too far from where the inn was under construction. Back then, it was a single-family home from a devoted husband to his cherished wife, or at least that was the story she told the guests.

"You've heard about our skeleton."

"Yep. Diamonds, too."

Over the last twenty-four hours, she had fantasized about having the missing diamonds, but Mark shot down that theory with all his information about diamonds having papers and people couldn't just show up at a jeweler with a handful of diamonds for sale. There were very few people who knew about the box besides herself and Mark. It wasn't likely the construction crew was calling Herman up. That left one person.

"I assume Ten called you."

"He did. He's a good one. Not sure if you know it, but he calls me every Saturday."

Ten makes a weekly call? It wasn't totally unbelievable since he had affection for the elderly man. Even though her employee might not be the most efficient worker, he did have a soft heart. It had been a little over a week since Herman and his buddies had descended on the inn for the wedding.

"Did he tell you we haven't opened the box yet?"

His exasperation carried over the phone line. "He did. What are you waiting for?"

"I know *you* would have pried it open by now, but Mark felt it's associated with the skeleton somehow and wanted to keep it intact for investigation. Besides, we've been busy. There's a Gen Con going on down here. Every room is booked. Mark and I had to give up our room. We're camping out at his old house that's stuffed with packed boxes and paint fumes. He's getting it ready for Detective Wells, that nice young man who helped with the high school reunion case."

"Another good one. It's always a pleasure to know your home will be in good hands. You think your mother might put me up?"

It sounded as if her old neighbor was ready to hit the road again.

Herman was allowed to leave the center, but his last trip involved springing three other residents of the home that didn't have the same rights. It would be best to nip it in the bud since Mark didn't have the time or the inclination to make sure they got back safely to Indiana.

"Maybe. You'd do better to ask her yourself. She likes you better than me." Herman's hoarse chuckle sounded as she expected. "As for the diamonds, they may not exist. Mark thinks the box is full of legal papers."

A derisive snort gave her a clue how Herman felt about that theory. The man had spent most of his life telling the tale of the mysterious jewel heist. Even though he had more than one version of the story, the G-rated one had the ne'er-do-well brother showing up with the diamonds. After a couple of drinks, Herman hinted that there was a love triangle. A jealous husband had murdered the jewel thief. In the end, the jewels were never recovered, which led their neighbor to insist they were still in Legacy or even in the inn. Donna wasn't a big fan of the stories since she had caught more than one guest thumping the walls looking for a hidden panel.

"I do wish you were here. Eventually, someone will have to figure out who the skeleton is. You're our neighborhood historian. If anyone would know if someone vanished in the last century, you would be my go-to person. As soon as we know the gender of the skeleton and a relative age, you can tell me anyone who has inexplicably disappeared."

Herman had always been a decent sounding board when she tried to work out crimes. Every now and then, he'd steer her in the right direction, even if she didn't always think so at the time.

"Glad to hear you say that. I'd be pleased to help."

"From a distance," she added, hoping to curtail any road trips.

"Please, Donna. You insult my driving skills. Anyhow, I'm in Ashville now."

The larger town was only a few hours away. Herman did have a niece and her family that lived there. "What are you doing in Ashville?"

"Big deal family reunion. Lois, my niece, is into the family tree stuff. Even sent off her DNA to get it analyzed. Anyhow, she found some more cousins and wanted to have a family reunion so everyone could meet them."

"How'd that go?"

"Painful. That branch of the family must have been pruned generations ago. Anyhow, Gwen, my grandniece, was going to drive me to Legacy since I flew in for the reunion. When I suggested it, she told me that she'd like to see Tennyson."

Donna rolled her eyes remembering how that ill-fated romance resulted in a morose employee talking about the futility of life. Since he had a girlfriend now, they could skip that part. Still, the last thing she needed was one more thing on her plate, but she had missed Herman. In some ways, he resembled her deceased father.

"You might try a day trip. With Gen Con going on, there will be a lot more cars and pedestrians, too."

"No worries. Gwen's driving. Since she's young, she has good reflexes. Not like me, when I have to tell my body to do something and often it replies with, 'What did you say?'"

Donna managed a forced chuckle, familiar with the man's humor. "Okay. They may have the entire skeleton by tomorrow. Then you can use that amazing memory of all things local."

"Looking forward to it, but not as much as I'm looking forward to you opening that box. See you soon."

He hung up before Donna could even reply. Even though there

was no one to hear her, she still said, "Bye."

Somehow, she needed to get Mark a heads up that Herman would be here. No way was she calling her husband and have him get his head bitten off again. The way things were going, she'd be awake by the time he got off shift, whenever that was. It would be hard going to sleep in a strange place. All the better for her to stay at the inn until she turned the door lock at ten pm. Hopefully, Maria informed the guests that they locked the door at ten. If anyone arrived later, Tennyson would have to unlock the door.

Some bed and breakfasts employed a keypad lock that guests could use to unlock the door after hours. What kept the guests from sharing the code? Maybe the other businesses changed it all the time, which would be a major pain. Most of their guests were not night owls and had no trouble getting back by ten. Somehow, she thought this time might be different.

Tennyson would be at the store picking up the groceries, which meant she'd have to be here. As long as she was, there were probably enough supplies to whip up a batch of cookies for Herman. An extra big batch could have her taking warm cookies into the dining room and engaging in some casual chit-chat. Unlike most folks, Donna could name every bone in the body and could connect them if need be. Although, the toe bones and finger bones did look rather similar.

By the time she had the oven preheating and the dough in the fridge to chill, Tennyson strolled into the kitchen with a triumphant look. He'd been gone for so long she couldn't remember what he left to do.

"I know something you don't know."

That was obvious since he had been gone forever. Unlike most men who could get by saying one word a day, Tennyson loved to talk. Sometimes she wondered if he initially chose philosophy as a major because it involved so much talking. Philosophers were always talking about what they believed and the nature of reality. No matter how long they talked, you still came away with the feeling that you had no clue what had been said.

"Is it about Joseph Carpenter?"

"No." He slid onto a bar stool and leaned his elbows on the island. "You're obsessed with that guy. I do know his team is freaking out because he was their leader and now there's some fighting about the tournament tomorrow."

"Really?" She hadn't even formed a theory of how someone who checked into an empty inn and tumbled down the stairs after an allergic reaction could not be a natural death. "Sasha told you this?"

"Not just Sasha. Thor and Giblet mentioned it, too."

"There's someone out there who named their child Giblet?"

Tennyson slapped the table. "You're such a jokester."

"No, I was serious. Living this far South, I've heard a few odd names. Folks like action names like Walker, Chase, and Runner. There's also the occupation names such as Doctor, Lawyer, Senator, and Governor, but I never heard of Giblet. Was his father a turkey?"

Instead of answering, Tennyson laughed so hard he wobbled on his stool. His hands wrapped around the seat to assure his position. Finally, he gasped, "No, that's a game name. Giblet is half dwarf and half goblin. See, the name makes sense."

"No, it doesn't." The oven chimed letting her know it had reached the right temperature. "Gorf would make sense."

"There's already a character by that name. He's part orc—"

Donna held up her hand to stop the recital of mythical creature bloodlines. "I don't want to know. Was Joseph a good player?"

"Apparently. Sasha thought they could have won the tournament."

Win the tournament. Maybe there was a great deal of money to be won. That would be motivation. So far, she hadn't convinced anyone that Joseph had been killed, not even herself. Still—she swung open the fridge door and grabbed the dough—something wasn't right about the whole thing.

"Is there money involved in the tournament?"

Tennyson had finally stopped laughing and scooted off his seat. He strolled over to where Donna was using a melon baller to make perfectly round scoops of cookie dough. He stuck a finger in the bowl and received a slight rap via the melon baller for his trouble.

"Ouch! I just wanted a taste."

"After they're done. There's raw egg in the mixture. You never answered my question."

His thin shoulders went up in a shrug. "Not really. There may be some merchandise given away, but that's it. Some D & D books and possibly some dice and cool figurines."

That didn't sound like anything anyone would be that concerned about. It did not sound like a motivation for murder—not like diamonds. "I guess they do it for the bragging rights."

"Possibly. They could do it for fun." His long finger pinched a bit of dough off a rounded cookie ball and shoved it in his mouth.

"Stop that!" She held up her melon baller as if a saber. Tennyson threw up his hands and walked backward a few steps.

"If you aren't nice to me, I won't—"

"Pick up my groceries." Donna inserted her own answer, because it was about that time.

His nose wrinkled as he regarded her. "I was going to say tell you about the skeleton, but get the groceries works, too."

Had something been discovered about the skeleton? It was way past time. Every time she checked they were very slowly putting the bones in a loose formation. Even though it had been years since anatomy class, Donna was sure she could have assembled the skeleton in under ten minutes. The three of them had been at it for over eight hours. "Well, don't just stand there. Tell me what it is."

Tennyson made a point of looking at the clock. "I better head out and get the groceries." He suited his actions to his words, causing Donna to chase after him. He'd reached the back stoop when he called back, "The skeleton is female!"

Her hand went up to her mouth, stopping whatever she might have said. A female skeleton totally skewed any of Herman's stories. What was a female skeleton doing next to her wine cellar?

Chapter Eleven

THE FRONT DOORBELL jangled as returning guests entered the inn, talking. Donna squatted by her stove, peering into the oven window, willing the cookies to cook faster. The sweet smell of warm macadamia and chocolate chip dough filled the kitchen. Bumping up the temperature would only singe the treat. They were her entrance to gab with the forensic crew. No one was ever thrilled to get burnt cookies.

With a sigh, she pushed herself to her feet. Couldn't stay in that position forever. Besides, everyone knew that a watched cookie never turned golden brown. Excited chatter filtered into the kitchen. There were breathless announcements about who was at the Con. The names meant nothing to Donna. It was hard for her to tell if the folks that caused so much excitement by merely showing up were celebrities or friends. A few talkers expressed their desire to do some Zelda live action role play game. That struck a bit of a responsive chord, but not enough to turn Donna away from her cookie watch.

The conversation was so loud they had to be standing almost next to the door. Since it sounded like other people had entered, they probably stepped to the side to let the new entrants go by.

One masculine guest spoke.

"We need to get to bed so we'll be on our A game tomorrow."

A game. She was familiar with the term, which usually meant doing your best, but it could also be a reference to just a regular game, too. The slow baking cookies no longer held her entire interest.

"What's the use, Henry?"

"Sasha. Remember we agreed to use our game names at the Con. Just because you chose to use your regular name for gameplay, doesn't mean the rest of us did likewise. I'm Thor, remember."

Even though Donna knew good and well she was eavesdropping, it didn't stop her from moving closer to the door. Her eyes rolled upward at the game name. He might as well have called himself Zeus, but she did notice from the spates of recent movies that there were none about any of the Greek gods or goddesses.

"Okay, Thor," the feminine voice overemphasized the name.

No need to see her face to tell that the woman was ticked off. Donna could imagine her throwing her hair back, if it were long enough to do so, and crossing her arms.

"Come on, guys." Another male voice intruded into the conversation. "We all miss Loki. It won't be the same without him. He was one of the best natural players I'd ever seen."

"I taught him everything."

"Really?"

The word practically dripped derision. If Thor couldn't hear it, there was no help for the man. Who was Loki? It was hard enough to sort the visitors out when they used their normal names, but why did they have to go and have game names? The tiny crack between the door and doorframe only allowed the tiniest peep. One of the males was tall and slender. He may have been the helpful one who carried her tray, but it was hard to tell with a one-inch view.

The red-headed girl was Sasha, of course. Her hair wasn't long enough to toss, but the angle of her shoulders indicated her arms could be crossed. The other fellow was short, stocky, and sported a full beard. If ever a person exemplified a dwarf, he was it. He could possibly be a gnome, too. Maybe he was Giblet.

The timer on the oven buzzed, pulling her away from the door. She made two long strides to the oven to rescue the cookies before they were overdone. Burnt cookies were bad, but the slightly overdone cookie that was hard when it should be soft made her sad. Although, it could be softened up if sealed up with a piece of fresh bread or a slice of apple, but that took time she didn't have.

It took a couple of minutes to transfer the cookies to the cooling racks. While the cookies cooled, she scooped another round of perfect spheres on the parchment paper lined cookie sheets. Instead of putting them in the oven, she opted for the industrial sized fridge because she couldn't count on how long she'd be casually chatting while delivering cookies.

The platter of cookies sent out an appetizing scent. Donna picked up the top one for a taste. After all, as a business owner, she had to sample the wares before presenting them. At least she did when it came to food. Testing out towels, hand soap, and fabric softener didn't have the same appeal as cookies.

It took both hands to carry the large platter, and she backed out carefully, wishing she had milk to go with the cookies. Coffee would have to do. As she drew close to the dining room, she announced in a forced cheery voice, "Who wants fresh baked cookies?"

The crew leaning over the skeleton looked up with expectant expressions. *Good.* Exactly what she wanted. Grateful people tended to be more mellow. The more mellow, the more they talked.

"I'll put them by the coffee. They're special macadamia chocolate chip. It's my own secret recipe."

Actually, she pulled the recipe from a cookbook and eliminated the cranberries and raisins that were originally in it since it felt too much like fruitcake to her. She had added a little nutmeg, turning it into her own concoction. She settled the cookies on the server and took a step back, waiting for the bone trio, who probably had germy hands.

Donna located a bottle of hand sanitizer and moved it by the napkins, hoping everyone would take a hint. If people chose not to use the sanitizer for whatever dumb reason, she couldn't be responsible for the outcome.

The two assistants moved first. Not exactly who she wanted, but they might be less guarded. "How's it going?"

Elle picked up a cookie without cleaning her hands, which made Donna cringe. "These are good. Are these vegan?"

That would be an answer she wouldn't like. "Tennyson told me the skeleton was female."

The older assistant, with the salt and pepper beard, had enough common sense to use the hand sanitizer. He nodded as if answering the question, then stacked three cookies on a napkin.

Elle opened her mouth to speak, but the sound of thundering footsteps on the stairs drowned out whatever she was going to say.

One voice carried over the sound. "See, I told you fresh baked cookies were just put out."

The herd stampeded into the living room like water buffalo and devoured the rest of the cookies. A few stopped for coffee. Donna had never seen water buffalo in full stampede, but had heard that of all the wild creatures, the water buffalo did the most damage. Or was it they caused the most deaths? The majority of the group left as quickly as they came, except for a few who rambled over to where Dr. Haddox was taking photos of the bones.

"Way cool. Is this some sort of puzzle or game?"

Before anyone could answer, the girl reached for a bone only to be smacked by Dr. Haddox. "No touch. Go away. Official business."

The girl tucked her smacked hand under her opposite arm. "There was no reason to resort to violence."

Instead of the smiling woman who was eager to tout her degree, Dr. Haddox directed a stare so icy it had to be a superpower. The girl backed up, grabbing her friend. and headed for the stairs.

At the moment, Donna wasn't so sure she wanted to talk to the doctor, either. She moved a little closer to Elle. "What did you say before the pillaging horde descended?"

"*We* determined the skeleton was female, around twenty."

The *we* comment earned her own frozen look from Dr. Haddox. She needed to get back into the kitchen and rustle up something for the woman to eat before she started munching on her assistants. Still, there was information here that Herman could use.

"You knew she was female from the pelvic girdle?"

"Yes, and the fact that her hand was still intact and there was an engagement ring on it." Elle wrinkled her nose. "It had a tiny diamond in it. More like a pre-engagement ring than an engagement ring."

"Not necessarily." Kelvin managed to talk around a mouthful of cookie. "Not everyone buys a flashy ring. Some people buy what they can afford."

Rather than dwell on the ring, or the size of it, she imagined a young woman who was excited about the prospect of being engaged, then ended up buried. It didn't sound right, but back in the good old days, even simple illnesses like the flu could wipe out an entire family.

"Do you have a clue how old the bones are? Not how old she was when she died, but how long they've been in the ground?"

Both assistants shook their heads as Dr. Haddox strolled over.

Her latex gloves gave a snap as she peeled them off. She picked up the thread of the conversation. "We can date with the condition of the bones plus geographic events that may have disturbed the bones. So far all we know is the bones were most likely interred close to a century ago. We could probably get an exact date if we had a peek into the box that was found with her. Surely that might have something dated inside. It could even hold a clue to her identity."

The crisp manner in which the statement was delivered sounded more like a demand for the box, which was still in Mark's trunk. Obviously, she couldn't provide the box immediately. It was her box, and if she chose not to show it to Dr. Haddox, all the better. A glance at her watch showed it was after ten. Past time the guests should be back and retired to their rooms.

"We'll talk about it in the morning." Donna delivered in her own no-nonsense tone. She refused to be pushed around in her inn, not that she was okay being pushed around in other places. She wasn't. Eleanor Roosevelt's famous quote was no one could make you feel inferior unless you let them. Her father's quote shaped her basic outlook on life with his "Stand your ground" philosophy.

The woman just stared at her. So, it was going to be that way. She'd give Haddox the benefit of the doubt and blame her attitude on being tired, but then again, Donna was tired. It might be a case of who was the crankiest. Well, she had cookies to finish and an inn to close up for the night. "I'm locking up the front door for the night." She angled her head the tiniest little bit as if to say do not mistake my exit for retreat.

The two assistants' heads swiveled between the two of them as if watching a tennis match. It was Dr. Haddox's turn to return the serve.

"Of course. I was wondering…" she lengthened the word, somehow gentling her tone in the process. Her lips tipped up into a questionable facsimile of a smile.

That must have cost her. "Yes?"

"Could you lock the dining room doors? You've already witnessed what could happen with so many curious eyes and fingers. Who knows if one of them might decide to take a souvenir?"

Her initial reaction was to point out that such a possibility was morbid, but she'd heard of average folks helping themselves to mementos that staggered common decency and sense. The woman had a point. Even if she closed and locked the pocket doors, anyone with a butter knife and a credit card could spring the lock, but she chose not to mention that fact.

"I could, but..." she hesitated just long enough to allow some tension to build, "I won't, since every guest here has paid for the privilege of breakfast. A real sit-down type of breakfast that will stick with them until they have to settle for a corn dog or whatever they'll be serving at the convention center."

Even the mention of event food reminded her of the jerk vendor who intimidated Maria until she put her heel to good use.

"What am I supposed to do?" The distraught woman threw up both hands while both assistants took a step away from her, which said a great deal.

If Mark were here, he'd be reminding Donna that she needed to play nice to this doctor who was fast turning into a diva when they needed her. "I could help you move the bones to your room. It would be the most secure place."

"Oh." Her eyebrows went up, and her mouth momentarily stayed in the O position. "We could do that. I use poster putty to keep the bones in place. If we hold the tablecloth tight it should work."

"You wouldn't have to worry about getting up so early, either."

Dr. Haddox just nodded.

It wasn't wild enthusiasm about the idea, but not total meltdown either. *Now, to seal the deal with a treat.* "I could bring you some cookies as soon as I get them baked."

"That would be acceptable." She gave two smart claps of her hands. "Let's go. We're moving the bones to my room."

Never mind that it was Elle's room, too. Donna wouldn't doubt that the young assistant would scamper around getting the doctor what she needed, from blankets to the remote, before being able to rest on her own rollaway cot. Tomorrow was another day, and she might end up meeting yet another Dr. Haddox. She'd already met the friendly professor and the demanding diva. Who knew who might make an appearance in the morning?

Not feeling like her presence was needed, she walked to the front door to lock it just when it popped open and vendor guy filled the entrance. *Oh, yay! He was still here.*

"I was about to close the door. If you arrive after ten, you have to ring the bell."

The man clutched his heart as if having a heart attack, then stumbled into the foyer. Just about when Donna was ready to swing into full nurse mode, he spoke.

"What is this place? Mayberry? Locking doors at ten pm?

Come to think of it, that old television show set in the fictional town of Mayberry did take place in North Carolina. "No, in Mayberry no one locked their doors. They only knocked because it was the polite thing to do."

"Well, I stand corrected. You'll be happy to know I left my van at the center since I scored a primo parking place. Took a cab back here."

At least that was one piece of good news. She'd text Maria to let her know Mr. Unsavory was still at the inn. Still, a guest was a guest, and this one might test her polite innkeeper banter. "Breakfast is between nine and ten."

The man had already turned and was on his way to the stairs as she spoke. *Rude.* He made an abrupt pivot to address her. "Did you say between nine and ten?"

"Did I stutter?" Someone needed to show up soon before she pushed her paying guest out the front door.

"Nope. Did you know most of your guests will already be at the convention since all the panels, workshops, even the vendor hall is open by nine?"

She hadn't. It wouldn't do much good to fix breakfasts for guest that weren't there. The fact that breakfast was included would cause some general grumbling in reviews if the guests didn't get one. In her opinion, most already had their meal allotment with the burgers and the cookies, but they wouldn't see it that way.

"Would breakfast from eight to nine work better?"

"Possibly. Better make it seven-thirty to eight-thirty."

If she served breakfast that early, she might as well sleep in her car. Maybe she could get by with breakfast sandwiches, fruit, and granola bars they could take with them. A sneaky suspicion worked its way into her mind. "What time are you leaving?"

"Not before seven-thirty, I don't want to miss out on someone else cooking for me."

Figures. She walked into that one. The man's mocking laughter trailed after him as he turned away to climb the stairs to the third floor.

Her hands rested on the small of her back as she tilted her head upward. "Have I been particularly bad lately?"

Here she tried so hard to be a kinder, nicer version of herself and she got Jerk the Vendor. Life wasn't fair. Joseph Carpenter or the girl buried with the tiny engagement ring could lecture about the unfairness of life. Right now, her job was to try to find some justice for both of them.

Too bad she didn't have a clue how she was going to do such a thing. Might as well do what she could do, and that was bake cookies. While she was at it, she'd poach eggs for in the morning.

Chapter Twelve

EVEN THOUGH DONNA'S plan had been to stay awake until her hubby came home, she fell asleep around one am watching some talk show that featured unknown movie stars talking about movies she had no interest in seeing. If the guests could have been a bit more interesting, she might have made it. Instead, she fell asleep with the bedroom light and television on.

A rocking sensation woke her up. At first, she thought she was back in her dream, paddling a flimsy canoe across the Pacific. The weary visage of her husband helped her to fix her actual location as being more ground-based as opposed to ocean-going. She rubbed her eyes, trying to bring everything into focus.

"What time is it?"

"Late or early depending on how you see it."

"Be serious."

"It is half-past three."

Donna moaned and flopped back on the mattress. She only had a couple more hours of sleep to go before she had to get up and hurry to the inn. If she were in her proper room, she'd get thirty more minutes.

"I didn't want to wake you, but you were mumbling something about not going to make it."

Remembering her dream, she grinned up at her husband. "I might be tired now, but if I had paddled all across the ocean, I would have been exhausted. Glad you woke me. How was the Con?"

"Yeah, that." He sat on the side of the bed and took off his shoes. "Looked like the attendees were having a good time. They came in chatty bunches, waving to people they either knew or wanted to know. It was hard to tell."

"We'll assume someone had fun." Donna pushed herself into a sitting position when she remembered hanging up on her hubby when the idiot in charge came along and started showing himself by micromanaging every officer and making jokes about Donna's sleuthing skills. "Sorry about hanging up on you, but I figured it was better that way."

He turned enough to wink. "Yeah, I hate to say it, but it was probably a good call."

Since she'd been asleep and paddling to China or somewhere, that meant there had been at least a couple of hours she hadn't considered the commissioner, but it all came rushing back. "Is no spouse or child of an officer ever supposed to call? There could be an emergency. A car wreck or something."

Her husband grumbled something under his breath as he unbuttoned his shirt.

"I didn't understand what you just said."

The shirt drifted to the floor as Mark bent to peel off his socks. "Just as well."

He walked over, turned off the television and light before unbuckling his pants, shedding them, and crawling into bed. His actions amused Donna a little. Before they married, she never would have pegged the man as bashful.

The springs complained a little as he settled into bed. "Why did you call me anyhow? I know it wasn't because you wanted to know how I was."

What had seemed imperative such a short time ago seemed rather silly now. Right before drifting off to sleep was the best part of her day, when the two of them would talk about their day and any secret dreams they might have. If she woke in the night and she could hear Mark's slight snore, her heart leaped. Since they'd hardly been married a week all the changes that occurred due to living with a man charmed her, except for the toilet seat being left up. That was a total deal breaker, which is why before the wedding, Mark installed a seat that gently closed itself.

"Why did I call?" She repeated the words aloud as if to jog her memory. "I wanted to know what Joseph's middle initial was."

"T." Mark rolled over and wrapped an arm around her waist, pulling her close to snuggle.

"Thanks," she murmured, enjoying the closeness. Even though the slightly bitter tang of sweat sat upon his skin, there was still the underlying essence that was uniquely her husband's. It would be easy to fall back asleep, lying content in his arms. His chest rumbled, signaling he was talking, but she couldn't quite decipher what he said. It was probably words of endearment she didn't want to miss since she had so few in her history. "Pardon?"

"There's no reason for you to be concerned about Joseph. His parents came and picked him up today."

The body was gone! She sat up, breaking out of Mark's loose embrace and turned on the light. "You let them take the body?"

"I had nothing to do with it. Apparently, his folks showed up while I was at the inn, flipping burgers for our hungry guests. Oscar handled it. As the coroner, he does that sort of thing without help or permission from me."

Her lips firmed into a line.

"Turn off the light and quit fussing. The boy died from natural causes. Peculiar, but that's all of it."

A twist of the light knob put them back into heavy darkness but did nothing to soothe her gut. She grabbed her pillow and shook it hard, fluffing it up. Then, gave it a couple of punches for good measure.

"Donna, please. If you hit that pillow one more time, we'll both be swimming in feathers. What's up with you?"

A body twist had her back to Mark. How could such an astute man sometimes be so clueless? His hand landed on her shoulder.

"Come on, honey, we're both too tired to play this game. Talk to me."

Her intention was to hold out longer, but she needed her sleep, too. "You're the one who wanted the CSI team, and now, nothing."

"I did want to turn over every stone. That is the type of police-man I was trained to be, but things are a-changing."

Donna waited in silence for him to say something else, but he didn't. Finally, she nudged him, which caused him to jerk, proving he had fallen asleep in mid-explanation.

"What do you mean things are *a-changing*?"

Mark yawned in her ear. "Do we have to have this discussion now?"

Donna reached for the lamp and turned it on, again causing Mark to groan. "We do if we both want to sleep in peace."

"I was doing fine until you elbowed me. You gotta remember that I'm no night owl."

"Things are a-changing," she prompted.

"Okay. The old-fashioned investigative work I used to do is no longer required. If people don't want it, we don't give it or even mention it. It's more cost-effective."

That was no type of police work. It sounded like pure laziness to her. "You've got to be kidding me. The mayor's okay with this?"

"Hard to say, but I told you before, I think Billings has something on the mayor. If we don't investigate crimes to their natural end, it will appear as if we have less crime, which in turn will make the commissioner and mayor look good."

Mark reached over her and turned the light off. He probably hoped he had turned off the discussion, too. If that was his intention, he was out of luck. The man she knew wouldn't simply follow orders *not* to investigate. "It's all a smokescreen. I can't believe you'd be a part of it."

Mark rolled over to his side of the bed and clicked on his bedside lamp. "I have no choice in the matter. Billings can fire me at any time, and he's looking for a trumped-up excuse to do so. I could lose my pension. Your goal was to have a bed and breakfast, and I want you to have it. One of us has to keep working a steady outside job to keep the inn going. Do you agree?"

"I do." She heaved a heavy sigh. "I don't have to like it though." She reached over Mark's prone body and turned off his light. "Go to sleep."

"It will be almost impossible with those wheels in your head grinding so loud. What proof do you have that Joseph Carpenter didn't stagger to the stairs, possibly in search of help for his allergic reaction, before falling down the stairs?"

A gut feeling never impressed anyone when it came to proof, but when a television cop went with it somehow things worked out. It might have something to do with the writers, too. She stared in the direction of the ceiling she couldn't see. Not being able to see it didn't make it any less there.

"I agree he had an allergic reaction and fell down the stairs."

"What's the problem then?"

"Timing."

"I'll bite."

"I knew you would." Her fingers located his arm in the dark and nudged him. "We were putting up the banner when we heard the scream. It might be slightly after we had the banner up since the dog walkers had to point out the misprint."

"I'm with you so far."

"Good." Over her pique, she snuggled into his side. Solving mysteries together was what they did best. People bond over different things. This was their thing. "We heard a scream."

"We assumed it was Joseph."

"I did at first, before I realized his throat and sinuses were swollen. It would have been hard for him to scream. Even if he had, we wouldn't have heard it. Someone else screamed."

Mark caressed her arm as he spoke. "Sweetheart, we discussed this before. I think we decided a workman saw him, screamed, and was unwilling to admit his actions."

That version she was on board with since she didn't want another murder at her inn. People die in hotels all the time. In the scheme of things maybe the inn would experience a natural death or two, but this felt wrong no matter how much she wanted it to be ordinary. It was a dull nagging pain that wouldn't go away until she solved it.

"Too much doesn't make sense. Tennyson may not be the most observant person in the world, but he would have noticed someone close to passing out. Joseph had to have been in acute distress when he checked in for his liver to be as cold as it was when the coroner examined him."

A wheezy snore sounded, proving all she had done was put her husband to sleep. Just as well. He'd ask about motivation, and so far, she had none. Since she didn't get to examine his suitcase, it was hard to say if there was any identification inside. The body had no cell or wallet, which was weird considering most millennials were more attached to their phones than their partners.

Maria probably put Kelvin into Joseph's old room. The police had no interest in it, which she'd thought was odd, but it could have been related to Gen Con. Legacy had somehow universally agreed to put everything on hold until Gen Con was over, allowing them to prove to anyone who was interested that they could host a convention just like the big cities. Maybe she should put everything on hold, too. *As if.*

Chapter Thirteen

THE EARLY MORNING dawn woke Donna before the alarm could. Not wanting to wake Mark, she crept out of bed and headed for the bathroom where she'd placed her clothes and toiletries the night before. At a quarter till seven, she scribbled a note telling Mark that coffee and breakfast would await him at the inn whenever he awoke.

On the way to the inn, she passed a few lone joggers in garish garb who might have been out-of-towners. It sure wasn't the takeover Mark and others had expected. An impulse had her driving past the convention center. The hotdog mobile was parked directly across from it. Next to it was a soft serve ice cream truck topped with a giant cone. Mariachi music came from another vendor with a banner that read "Best Tacos Anywhere." A car towing a pushcart vehicle attempted to maneuver into the open parking slot. *Good luck with that, friend.* Parallel parking was never one of her strong suites.

Seeing what the attendees had to pick from as far as food went made Donna even more determined to make sure everyone had a nutritious breakfast. As she slowly worked her way out of the congested area, she spotted Officer Wells who was already on duty.

She beeped her horn and powered down the window and stopped to chat. "What are you doing here so early?"

"It's the shift I pulled."

"You do know nothing starts before 9 am?"

"That's what I heard. At least I'll get home at a decent time, not like Mark." He shook his head.

"Yeah, what's up with that?"

Wells shrugged. "Dunno. It's hard to miss that Billings is gunning for Mark. It rubs us all the wrong way. We'll remember this at the upcoming election."

"I know I will. See ya."

Donna waved before she powered up the window and drove away. It didn't make sense that a mayor would appoint a wildly unpopular commissioner during an election year. It could be that he underestimated the locals' reaction to an out-of-towner. If there were enough disgruntlement, maybe the mayor would lose the election. A different candidate would pick a different commissioner. It sounded like a mission to her as soon as she sent the skeleton on its way and unraveled the mystery of Joseph. If he were a D & D player, he would have a name. Wonder if it had anything to do with a unicorn?

The coffee was brewing, and Maria looked up from adjusting the preheat button on the oven.

"Morning, Donna. I hustled over here since I knew you'd have to drive across town."

"It wasn't too bad."

"I already have some fruit and bagels out along with cream cheese and peanut butter since I didn't know when everyone would get up."

"Good deal." Donna put her purse on the hook and bent down to greet Jasper. As she washed her hands she remembered the jerk vendor. "I think you should know that hot dog guy is still here. No reason for you to go into the dining room. I suspect he'll leave early to snag those folks who didn't have sense enough to book a B and B."

"Thanks for the warning."

The door creaked as Tennyson entered. The deep circles under his eyes hinted at a restless night.

"Was there some movie marathon on last night?" Donna asked.

His lips firmed into a line before he answered. "I wish. I didn't get to bed until midnight. Those bone folks wanted extra pillows, washcloths, and heavy-duty soap to get the clay off."

None of the requests were that unusual except for the time they were given. "You should have gotten at least six hours, which is pretty decent."

"I'd have been happy with six." He peeked into the bread baskets to see if the pastries had been put in yet. They hadn't.

Donna pulled out the English muffins, cheese, and Canadian bacon to assemble her sandwiches. First, she had to warm up the eggs she'd poached last night. Maria opened the oven as she hefted the tray from the fridge. As Donna bent to push in the heavy tray filled with water and eggs, Tennyson spoke.

"The parties were what kept me awake. Doors slamming. Music, laughter, and shouting. Doesn't anyone sleep anymore?"

At the mention of parties, her grip slipped a little, but fortunately, the pan was already on the rack, and only a minuscule amount of water splashed onto the heating elements with a sizzle.

Donna straightened and landed a censorious look on her employee "What parties?

He held up his hands. "I had nothing to do with it."

"You didn't stop it?"

"I didn't know how. I heard the doors slamming, and by the time I went out to look, especially since I had to climb the stairs, there was no one about. Couldn't tell who was doing what. Room parties are kind of a thing when you have these types of conventions."

Donna sighed and placed her hand on her lower back, which ached due to a night spent on an uncomfortable mattress. "I wish you would have told me about the parties."

"You never asked."

"True." She shouldn't have to ask about everything. Unfortunately, people assumed she knew things that she didn't. "Things didn't get out of hand, did they?"

The thought made her want to rush through the rooms, checking the floors and furniture for half-empty beer bottles and crumpled snack bags. Every piece of art, every runner, every estate sale piece of furniture was an investment. Sometimes, she labeled things by how many hours she worked to earn the money for it. There was her subzero fridge that took four double shifts and giving up most of her vacation days.

She started for the dining room, but Tennyson stopped her. "It's okay. I've already been upstairs. I've walked through the place and didn't spot any broken beer bottles or confetti. Figured I might as well since that dude woke me up bringing down his jumbo cooler. Not even sure why he needed a cooler that large."

Pulling out a cooler in the middle of the night was weird. "Did you ask him why he was moving the cooler out in the middle of the night?"

"No. I just peeked out my window and saw him loading it into his car. I didn't confront him. He was probably sneaky about it since he didn't know how you might feel about bringing food and stuff to drink in. I made sure to lock the door after he came back in."

Donna would have had no issues with confronting sneaky cooler guy. "Do you know who it was?"

"Just some guy. I was going on the silhouette. I guess it could have been an athletic girl, considering how much trouble he or she had carrying the cooler. I swear it must have banged on the floor every step."

Donna pressed both hands to her chest. "Oh, my precious hardwood floors!"

"You have runners on the stairs," Maria reminded as she placed the pastries on cookie sheets to warm.

"You're right." She turned to look at her sister-in-law. "Do you remember someone coming in with a huge cooler?"

"There were some coolers, but they were little ones that you'd used for a six pack or sandwiches. Can't recall any larger ones. Still, a person could have checked in, then gone out to their car to get a cooler when I was in the kitchen."

"You're right." Instead of the issue of a cooler being settled, it nagged at her all through breakfast. They got most of the conventioneers out by nine, which was about the time the bone crew arrived to dine.

Fortunately, they were okay with breakfast sandwiches, too. Tennyson had already loaded the dishwasher, and Maria had taken off her apron when Mark arrived.

"Hello. Looks like I missed the breakfast rush, and now you're leaving?"

Maria replied. "You missed the rush all right. I need to go home and take care of Cici. Daniel has a list of sites he needs to inspect. He decided he would wait until later to do them. I'm sure he'd look very authoritative with a baby in one arm."

Mark chortled. "Well, I guess you better go then."

Greetings were given all around before Maria ducked out the door. Donna poured a cup of black coffee and placed it on the island surface for her husband.

"I see you saw my note."

"I did." He gave her a brief kiss before picking up the coffee cup and inhaling deeply. "I need this."

Her hand rested on the nearby barstool as her eyes roamed over his face. A yellowish tinge colored his skin, making her draw on her medical resources. "You getting enough water? Maybe you're dehydrated? Vitamin B12 deficiency?"

He took a healthy swallow of coffee, then gave an approving sound. "Donna, I was in an air-conditioned building all night."

"True, but before you left, you slaved over the grill making those burgers. You don't look good. You're yellowy."

His hand covered his mouth as he yawned. "I was warned the romance would stop once I said *I do*, but now you're telling me I don't look good."

"Ha-ha! You know what I mean. You're still your handsome self, but something's off. The color could indicate a multitude of disorders. Even hepatitis, jaundice, cancer of the small intestine."

"Please. If you're trying to cheer me up, stop. I'll tell you what's wrong."

Donna slipped into the stool beside him. "Go on."

"It's all this BS that Billings is spreading around. I've swallowed so much it's no wondered I'm turning colors. He told Clinton, the officer whose wife is nine months pregnant, that he couldn't leave just because his wife called. She had to be at the hospital and in active labor before Clinton could go."

Just when she thought Billings couldn't sink any lower in her opinion, he did. "I don't get it. He doesn't want you to actively investigate incidents, then he has you all standing around an empty convention center. I saw Wells on my way in, standing duty outside an unoccupied building. Now Clinton isn't allowed to drive his wife to the hospital? What does your union rep have to say about this?"

Her husband gave her a long stare, jogging her memory. "Oh yeah, you don't have a union."

Mark reached for his cup and stared into it. Donna grabbed his empty cup with the intention of filling it but placed it back on the island surface. "You need food, not coffee. With all the stress you're under, you'd be better off having milk."

"Milk!"

Tennyson entered the room carrying the tray of juice and milk decanters. "You're in luck, we still have some. The orange and cranberry juice are gone, but there's plenty of skim and low-fat milk left." He placed the tray on the island and handed Mark the milk containers.

"Ten, you need to get Mark a big glass for his milk," she said, taking quick advantage and smiling as she centered the Canadian bacon on his muffin bottom. Her husband wouldn't refuse something Tennyson offered him. Since the rush was over, she fixed herself a sandwich, too. Today, the egg muffin sandwiches went over well. Tomorrow, she'd have to come up with something else that was portable.

Not to laugh at the sight of her husband morosely staring at the tall glass of milk Ten filled was hard as she set both plates on the island and took a seat. "Here we go. We have some fruit in the dining room. At least, I think we do."

His fingers wrapped around the still warm sandwich. "This is plenty. It's certainly better than the sludge coffee and stale donuts I survived on before I met you."

She closed her eyes and shook her head, not even wanting to think about it. "It's amazing you survived."

"Cold pizza and cigarettes made me who I am today." He

smirked, daring Donna to say something.

"That's why you almost ended up spending Christmas in the cardiac unit."

The back door slammed, and a voice called out, "Sounds like the lovebirds are cooing to each other."

Both Mark and Donna turned in unison as an elderly man with a thick mane of silver hair strolled into the kitchen. "Herman!"

Chapter Fourteen

AFTER HUGGING HERMAN, Donna noticed Gwen, his grandniece, who had driven him to Legacy. Even though the romance that Ten thought existed between him and Gwen may never have happened outside of his imagination, Donna found it hard to feel very loving toward her, after weeks of whining and depression from Ten when she left. Thank goodness for Sloane. Ten's current squeeze snapped him out of that awful funk. Still, southern hospitality was expected. She'd offer the Devil sweet tea if he showed up at her door. Donna would bring it out, though, as opposed to inviting him in.

She nodded in Gwen and Herman's direction. "You hungry?"

A look of expectation stretched across Herman's face as he rubbed his hands together. "Sweeter words were never spoken."

"Uncle Herman, we ate before we left Ashville."

"That's been forever ago. Sit down, Gwen, and have some real food."

They both sat as Donna bustled around the kitchen, only sorry she didn't have anything more elegant for her old neighbor. "I can make some fruit crepes if you're willing to wait."

"The ones with that sweet lemon sauce?"

Since she had all the required ingredients, it was feasible. "Yes."

"Sounds great." He gave his niece a nudge. "You're going to appreciate this. There's nothing quite like home cooking."

Gwen elbowed him back. "That's not what you said at the family reunion."

Herman groaned and caught Donna's eyes. "Here I have all these folks in my family and what do they bring to the reunion, but stuff they bought at the grocery deli. None of that stuff is fit to eat." He gave Mark a pat on the shoulder. "You lucked out snatching up one of the few women that still cooks."

Mark agreed while Donna whipped up the batter, amused at her former neighbor's enthusiasm for her cooking. This is what running an inn was supposed to be like. It wasn't late night room parties and clunking an oversized cooler down the steps. She hadn't even mentioned the cooler to Mark yet.

A chiming cell phone had the two of them patting down their pockets. Mark pulled out his phone and flourished it to show it was the ringing one.

"Taber here."

Donna couldn't hear the other end of the conversation, so she tried reading her husband's expressions to determine what was happening. No brow lowering, which was good. His tone remained normal, another good sign. He continued to speak.

"Understand. I'll be there in a little bit."

That wasn't what she wanted to hear. The man just got up after dragging himself home after three in the morning. She waited until he pocketed his phone. "You'll be where?"

"At the convention center. Clinton's wife just went into labor, so I'll take his shift. You should be glad. That means I won't be crawling home in the wee hours. After eleven last night, there really wasn't anything happening. I did have two guys who sat on the steps arguing about the merits of classic Star Trek over the newer versions."

It wasn't what she wanted but being there for his co-workers defined who Mark was. "First, you're going to finish your breakfast and your milk."

"Yes, ma'am. What if I told you I was lactose intolerant?"

Donna knew better but decided to play along. "I guess there will be no more cheesecake in your future."

He picked up the glass of milk and chugged it. "Could you find me one of those insulated coffee cups to take with me?"

"I can." She mentally added, *and I'll fill it up with decaf, too.*

Knowing he had a limited time before Mark left, Herman spoke rapidly, rehashing news of his cold crimes club at the center. He and a handful of his friends had been solving crimes that had long since been put aside.

Gwen, probably familiar with the story, interrupted. "What's going on down at the convention center? Last time I was here it wasn't even finished."

"Gen Con," Mark answered before he bit into his sandwich.

"Here?" Gwen looked puzzled as if she hadn't heard right. Ten chose that moment to wander into the room. No dramatic chord of music sounded. They both nodded to each other in recognition, but that was it.

As the youngest person in the room, Ten might have felt the need to explain. "It's not a big Gen Con. It's one of the smaller ones, but we got it due to the other city having bed bugs."

Even though it was the truth, it certainly sounded less grand delivered in such a prosaic manner. Gwen acted interested. "Have you gone?"

"Not yet. I've been needed here."

It had never occurred to her that Ten even wanted to go. "Once we finish cleaning up the breakfast mess, you're welcome to check it out. Maybe you could pick up Sloane."

"That would be fun." She arched her eyebrows and pressed her hands together. "Sloan is such a fun person."

No worries there. She should put her energy into real issues. In less than ten minutes, she sat down to watch Herman enjoy his crepe, while Ten and Gwen finished up the last dishes together in an effort to get down to the convention center faster.

The two of them waved and called out in unison, "See ya."

Donna returned their waves, wondering when she had ever been that excited about going somewhere.

Herman cut a bite of crepe and put it into his mouth. He closed his eyes and moaned. "Oh, this is heaven. It almost brings tears to my eyes."

Most people liked her cooking, but when you came right down to it, no one truly loved it as much as Herman. The man truly experienced her food. "Thanks. I love cooking for those who like eating."

"Well, that would be everyone."

"No. Some people do it just to stay alive. They don't enjoy it like you do."

He put down his fork long enough to hold up one finger. "Most of the stuff they fix at the center is bland and tasteless. I can't see anyone enjoying that. If the elderly are supposed to have diminished taste buds, why not use more flavoring as opposed to less?"

Feeling that it was a rhetorical question, she settled on a simple shrug. "I would like to use you as a sounding board, though. I'd tell you what I know about the skeleton, then I'll give you the details on the suspicious death that happened at the inn."

"Another one?" Herman picked up his fork and went back to devouring the crepe.

"Afraid so. First, I should tell you about the skeleton. So far, they know it is female, around twenty, wearing a small pre-engagement or engagement ring. We're assuming since she was under the foundation, she must have been placed there about the time the house was going up."

The metal tines of the fork scratched the plate as Herman rounded up his last morsel and popped it into his mouth. Finally, he patted his stomach and looked around the kitchen. "Where's that fancy coffee pot?"

"In the dining room. I'll check and see if we have any coffee left."

There was enough for another couple of cups, which pleased her since she never liked wasting anything. When she entered the kitchen, Herman's head was angled down. It was hard to tell if he was asleep. "Are you okay?"

He glanced up. "Technically, yes. The skeleton, being a female, ruins my jewel thief theory."

"Not necessarily. Women can commit crimes, too. At the time, they'd be less likely to suspect a woman. She might have even had a better chance to get into wherever the jewels were on exhibition. She could have been a maid or even a visitor."

"Yeah, I can see that. What about the ring?"

"I've given that some thought." When she wasn't hating on Billings and trying to construct a backstory for Joseph that is. "I thought she was engaged at first, then maybe she got sick. People died all the time a hundred years ago. It wouldn't have even been odd for them to inter her in the basement or farm or what it was at the time."

Herman picked up the coffee that she prepared just as he liked it and took a sip. "Now, I know everyone considers me the neighborhood historian. My house," he gestured to the window where his former house could be seen through the sheers, "was one of the first built in this area. We have old sepia photos of my parents on this property. According to my father, it was a type of park with a few benches and a walking path. He used to play here with his little bulldog. It may have belonged to the city. I suspect no one would have been buried on the property. At least not with anyone knowing. Whatever happened had to be secretive. It makes more sense that this woman was buried while the building was going up."

"I think part of it goes back to what is in the box."

They were back to the box again. The same mysterious box that was somewhere in Legacy. If it were truly valuable and an opportunist knew about it, Mark's trunk would be history. "If you insist on seeing the box, we might get it open today."

Herman slapped the table. "That's the whole reason I came down here. Well, and to see ya'all, of course." He managed a sheepish expression. "Now, tell me about your suspicious death."

She held her hand up. "Listen to the whole story before making any snap judgments. This guy shows up at the hotel a day early. Ten waits on him and never makes eye contact because he has a knit hat that covers his hair and sunglasses. A short time later, we're all outside looking at the banner—"

"About the banner—"

"I know." Donna heaved a disgusted snort. If even Herman could see the mistake, then it was obvious. "We hear a scream, run in, and Joseph is dead at the bottom of my stairs with a unicorn mask on his head."

"Unicorn mask?" Herman's bushy eyebrows went up in inquiry.

"I'm not done, so hold your questions. Anyhow, Mark and I tried to save him, but it's too late. When I cut the mask off the man, Ten tells me he's not sure if it's the same person who checked in. Fingerprints confirmed it was Joseph Carpenter. The coroner shows up, tells us the man died from an allergic reaction and must have tumbled down the stairs. However, his liver was too cool for his time of death."

"Something is afoot. What happened then?"

Even though Herman had interrupted again, she decided not to point it out since he was the only person willing to listen to her tell the entire story. "I took some photos. Wells went upstairs, got the man's suitcase, and the coroner sent the body to the county morgue. His parents took the body and suitcase away. So, what do you think?"

Herman picked up his coffee for a sip, then regarded it with a disappointed mien. "Sounds to me like the fellow died from an allergic reaction and tumbled down the stairs."

Here she was counting on Herman to see the inconsistencies in the narrative. "Did you miss the part about him screaming?"

"Heard it."

Donna shook her head slowly, bewildered why she couldn't get anyone else to see what she saw. "His throat and sinuses were swollen due to the allergic reaction. He wouldn't have been able to scream. However, we heard a definite scream."

"Peculiar."

"Then, Ten wasn't sure if it was the same person."

"It would have to be. Who else could it be?"

"Someone pretending to be Joseph Carpenter to set the scene for an accidental fall down the stairs."

Herman laid a finger beside his nose. "We can agree Ten is a sweet boy, but not the most observant. Still, wouldn't he have noticed if whoever checked in was lugging around a dead body? Besides, when had anyone used an allergic reaction as a murder weapon?"

"It happens more than you might think, but the murderer has to know the victim is allergic. It could be a family member or friend."

Herman harrumphed as his eyes rolled upward. "Okay, I'll give you the allergic reaction is odd, but you had no way to lug a body upstairs and no motivation. Maybe it was just an accident."

Both of her hands covered her face. Why couldn't she get someone to believe her?

Chapter Fifteen

A DISTINCTIVE KNOCK, then the clang of the back door as it opened and shut brought Donna's head up fast. The force of nature known as her *mother* had arrived.

"Hello, all!" Cecilia called out as she removed oversized sunglasses that made her resemble Jackie Onassis. Her current gentleman admirer, Simon, followed behind her rather like a tugboat in the wake of a mighty ocean liner.

"Hi." Donna couldn't help noticing her mother had on a lovely floral sundress, cut conservatively for the mature woman, paired with dainty sandals and an oversized sun hat. When people saw mother and daughter together, she assumed they were a little disappointed that the fashion gene had skipped a generation. Maybe she took after her father in that matter. "It's great seeing you, but a surprise."

Tinkling laughter sounded—another thing Donna hadn't inherited-as her mother fluttered her fingers.

"Oh, baby. I had to come and see Herman while he was in town. We bumped into Gwen and Ten down at the center."

They were at Gen Con? Even though she never attended a convention, Donna assumed it was something those under thirty did. There'd be no bouncer who sent you on your way if you weren't the right age, but there could be judgmental stares that would have those who didn't fit rushing to the door. "How was it?"

Her mother threw a smile at Simon, who answered for her. "Delightful. There was a live chess game going on with people playing the parts of chess pieces."

"Sounds interesting." Donna wasn't sure if she wanted to play chess publicly, allowing others to take note of her lack of strategy. Still, it wasn't what she expected as far as the convention.

"Too bad you missed it." Simon grinned as he explained. "The people were dressed as chess pieces. The knight had on one of those Halloween costumes that made him appear to be riding a horse with a horn."

A unicorn. Weird. Did that have anything to do with Joseph? "What else did you do?"

Cecilia nodded at her beau and picked up the conversational thread. "We played this video game where each person controlled their character up on screen. That's where we met Gwen and Ten."

The idea of her mother sitting down with a video controller in her hand boggled her mind, especially since the woman had resisted using a cell phone until a few years ago. Both Mom and Simon beamed as they explained what they'd been up to. After her father died, she and her brother worried about their mother being alone and bereft for a few months. She always knew her mother was the quintessential southern woman, able to flatter any man into doing distasteful jobs, dress like she stepped out of a genteel ladies' magazine and make sweet tea with one hand while delivering an insult without it sounding like one to an unwelcome caller. That was her mother.

The only skill her mother didn't have that most women her age could lay claim to was cooking. Donna's talent in the kitchen came from the desire to actually eat something tasty. Her mother's tired selection of cereal and Hamburger Helper inspired Donna to pick up a cookbook. By simply following directions, a delicious dish resulted. Even though the young Donna tried to interest her mother in the joys of following directions, her efforts were far from successful. Often the noodles in their cheeseburger casserole were still crunchy because Cecilia failed to time them.

Both she and her brother followed their father's lead by eating and not complaining. Most would have called such behavior a courtesy, but it may not have been that. Any hint that her cooking was less than acceptable would have ended up with her father fixing supper, which wasn't an outcome he desired, although Donna couldn't see how he could be any worse. Her mother loved trying new things, except in the kitchen.

"Tell me about the game?"

Simon chuckled. "Your mother was supposed to be a communi-cation officer and give the other players information."

Donna nodded, aware there was a silent '*but*' added to the sentence. Before Simon could finish, Cecilia did. "Oh, mercy me, I didn't know I was supposed to do that! Sounds rather boring."

Typical. There were always proper ways to do things. Via her mother, she'd heard more than a dozen times how to greet someone, the proper form for a thank you note, and how to address the Queen if she should ever pop into Legacy while on one of her horse-buying trips. Even though Cecilia Tollhouse's world was composed of endless rules, she reserved the right to break any of them when she felt like it and it served her purpose.

"Goodness," her mother drawled and waved her free hand as if she had a lace handkerchief and was signaling to the world at large how dainty and feminine she was. "I just shot everyone."

"Including me," Simon pointed out. "It was a very short game."

That Donna could well imagine, and no one could truly be mad at her mother since her intentions were good, although that might not apply at the convention. "No one was upset you shot them by accident?"

"It was deliberate. I always wanted to try my hand at one of those first-person shooter games."

It may not have been a first-person shooter game, but Donna was enjoying the interaction between Cecilia and Simon. It was so hard for the beau not to correct her mother. Among the seventy and older set, her mother was a catch. In a candid moment, Simon had admitted to having a crush on Cecilia in high school, which forced him into a complicated wooing that resembled herding cats. As far as she knew no one ever herded cats successfully. Only one man ever won the heart of Cecilia Tollhouse, but Simon might be the second.

Herman agreed. "Me, too. They have some video games at the center that you can play in the lounge on the big screen, but they involve things like having a virtual family or running an island. Don't they have a clue we're at the age that we want to have fun? Race cars. Win wars. Chase bad guys and occasionally be the bad guy."

"I hear ya." Simon stepped forward and slapped the former neighbor on the back. "Maybe you'd like to join us later. Cecilia and I signed up to do an escape room game, but we need a team. They just don't let two people in at a time. We need four or possibly six."

"Sounds interesting. I need to meet the skeleton lady first."

It was hard to tell if he was referring to the forensic scientist or the skeleton. It was sweet Simon invited Herman to join them, but that only made three. They'd need at least one more. She should make a quick survey of the rooms for the most welcome sign of all, the *do not disturb* one hanging from the doorknob. Half the time, people forgot they left it on the door when they returned to an unmade bed and wet towels on the floor. If there was some partying going on, as Ten supplied, there would probably be several signs on the doors.

While sometimes she had negative opinions of guests, it worked the other way, too. Guests sometimes used the sign to keep the maid, which was Donna, out. She wasn't sure what they were more afraid of, her pawing through their lingerie, sampling their liquor, or judging their shoe choices. A nosy person might do that. She was strictly business, but sometimes that business was sleuthing.

"Let me go check the rooms first. What time did you reserve the escape room?"

Her mother had her shopping bag on the island and scattered colorful hats and props, which she was showing Herman. Cecilia glanced up and made a moue with her lips. After an awkward silence ensued, she finally spoke. "I didn't think you'd be interested."

Obviously, she hadn't been invited. How could her mother ditch her? "Why wouldn't I be interested?"

"Well, ah…" Her mother reached for a scepter topped with a bright red heart and a golden cardboard crown dotted with little hearts. "You have to wear a disguise to participate. I'm going as the queen of hearts." She pulled off her sunhat and replaced it with a crown.

Simon donned an oversized hat proving what character he would be. While Herman put on a headband with an oversized bow for Alice. Costumes were going fast as she racked her brain about what other characters were in the story. A suspicion grew as she checked all the trio wearing silly hats. None of them looked as if they were having fun, instead, they looked apprehensive.

"You didn't ask me because you didn't think I would be fun."

Her mother cut her eyes to Simon, silently swearing him to

secrecy before turning back to face Donna. "It's not that, sweetie. You have so much on your plate right now."

"Admit it. You don't think I'm fun." Normally, fun wasn't how she'd categorize herself. But now—when she realized no one regarded her as a frivolous lightweight who'd don a costume in a New York second to play a stupid game-she wanted it.

Her mother reached for an oversized rabbit head that would cover her face and hair and held it out to Donna. Her fingers wrapped around it, finding it surprisingly light for its size. "Why can't I wear the headband? I'm a natural blonde, which would make me a better Alice."

Herman slapped his hands over the sides of the headband as if afraid Donna would snatch it from his head. "I was asked first, which meant I got first pick. I'm not giving up my headband." He waggled his bushy brows. "Besides, I always wanted to see what it would be like to be female for a change."

Not believing the statement, she took a deliberate step back. "I don't want to be too close when you're struck by lightning."

Her mother clapped her hands together. "You take things too seriously, which is why I didn't ask you in the first place. Wear the rabbit head if you want to be part of our group."

Cat ears and a tail were left on the island surface. Donna made a grab for then, but Cecilia knew her well and grabbed them before she could. "Mom! Why can't I be the cat?"

"Are you willing to be silent the entire game and just smile? That's what the Cheshire cat does."

While not a fan of Lewis Carroll books, she found it hard to believe the cat did not talk. Why have it in the story? "Are you sure the cat never talks?"

"Mostly never. He does tell Alice everyone in the story is crazy, then smiles away. That's all you get is one line, then you have to smile for sixty minutes."

That sounded like torture. "You want me to wear the rabbit head because no one else will."

Cecilia lifted her chin a little, a classic move when she didn't have a fast rebuttal. As an extrovert, her mother had a quiver full of humorous zingers. "Personally, as a businesswoman, I would have thought you wouldn't want to be seen by your guests engaging in a silly game."

Oh, she knew what her mother was doing. The hospital staff might think she was good at getting people to do what she wanted, but she was a novice compared to her mother. Rather than tackling the issue of the giant rabbit head with the scary teeth, she focused on the mention of the guests being there. At least some of the guests knew Joseph Carpenter. Maybe while at the con she could duck into the D & D tournament. Would it look odd if she still wore the rabbit head? Even if it did, no one would recognize her with the head on. "I'd love to be the rabbit."

Cecilia, who chatted with Simon, did a double take. "You would?"

"Sure." She managed a wide grin that would confuse her mother even more. "Sounds like a great part. What are my lines?"

"Didn't I ever read you the story?"

"No. You taught me how to read when I was four so you wouldn't have to read to me. I chose books that would be more of a practical use, such as books about animals and seasons."

"Even at four, you were already practical. As for your lines, you say "I'm late. I'm late for a very important date.""

That was lame. No wonder she'd never bothered to read the book. "Got it. When is our game time?"

"It's at 1 pm." Her mother held up her wrist decorated with a slim watchband as if Donna could read that across the room. Instead, her eyes went to the wall clock that showed she had ninety minutes to clean up and be ready to go. She also knew the inn would not remain empty of its curious guests for long, which meant she would need to call in Maria to fill in for her if she headed down to the convention center.

"All right, let's check the dining room and see if our bone people have brought the skeleton out."

The tarp stretched over her large dining table as Dr. Haddox pushed a bone into place. The light clatter of fingers on the keyboard signaled Elle was typing something while Kelvin took photos of the entire procedure for a digital record for their own research, or it might show up in a promotional folder for forensic science.

"Hi, all!" she called out and realized only after she did it that she had copied her mother's greeting.

The trio stopped their work and glanced back at them. With most of Donna's appearances usually coinciding with food delivery, Elle's hopeful expression may have meant she'd welcome a break or a snack. Kelvin acted baffled that other people were even at the inn, but there was no mistaking Dr. Haddox's expression. Had the woman forgotten this was her inn? If anyone was inconvenienced, it was Donna. While Dr. Haddox got to play the part of Goldilocks sleeping in the bed that was just right, Donna breathed in paint fumes all night to accommodate her.

The tight-lipped smile Dr. Haddox offered both Cecilia and Simon when introduced all but shouted *be gone*. The blue latex gloves remained on her hand, and she made no effort to remove them and shake hands. Yesterday, the anthropologist was much friendlier, but that may have been before she got her hands on the bones. Now, she could be in total work mode and resented the interruption.

Knowing Herman would know more about the bones than anyone, she wanted a little more respect from the woman. "This is Herman, who has lived in the house across the street since he was a child. His father before him lived in the same house and played on these grounds when it was a park. Herman knows all the history associated with the area."

"Is that so?" She pulled off the rubber glove from her right hand and held it out. "Pleased to meet you. I am sure you've heard about the skeleton. Do you have any theories?"

As Herman warmed up to his multiple theories, she herded her mother and Simon into the parlor. "Call Maria and see if she can babysit the bone crew while we go play the game. Have her come early, and you can have some facetime with your grandbaby."

Her mother already had her phone out as she hit the stairs at a jog. She should have asked Tennyson to stay and help, but since there were so few things that ever happened in Legacy, it didn't feel right denying him the opportunity to check out the convention, especially now since she'd be doing the same thing, only she'd be investigating. The rabbit head would be her deerstalker hat. If luck were with her, there'd be no stairs involved in the escape game.

Chapter Sixteen

THE SUNLIGHT POURED through the car glass window blinding Donna as she tried to peer out. There was a blare of horns, which made her wince with her mother at the wheel. Simon Lightwater was enough of a traditionalist to drive her mother everywhere, but he'd bought a new car, which to most would not seem like a big deal. The sharp looking luxury crossover vehicle had her mother begging to drive it. Like any besotted suitor, he agreed, possibly thinking what could happen?

Some would be happy not knowing what was going on as her mother weaved through traffic. Instead of mentally tracing the path to the center and how many times she could die in the process of getting there, she should relax into the plush seats and converse with Herman. One look at her ashen-faced former neighbor, whose left hand gripped the panic strap for dear life, squashed that idea.

By this time, Simon may have realized that Cecilia was not your typical little old woman driver. Oh no, she had a hankering for things that went fast. Most local men enjoyed the car races. Her father hadn't. That didn't mean the television wasn't tuned to the races with Cecilia yelling instructions to the drivers, convinced if they'd listen to her they'd win. The only problem with a wannabe race car driver tendency, besides other vehicles on the road, was her mother's insistence on turning to look at someone when she talked to them. Good manners dictated you looked someone full in the face or at least tried to.

Donna's finger stabbed at the window release powering it down. A wave of sound pushed in along with the hot humid air.

"Roll up the window. The air is on," her mother urged as she twisted in her seat to do so, causing the car to swerve to the right, narrowly missing a parked car. Simon reached for the wheel and corrected it.

Her mother gave him a slight tap as he held onto the wheel. "Simon, please. I know what I'm doing."

The man let go of the wheel, probably a little reluctantly. This incident might spell the end of their romance. What Simon didn't know is Cecilia thought she was incapable of wrecking, which explained her reckless driving skills. Folks in Legacy gave those less than wonderful skills a wide berth. Since her father had handled most of the driving before he passed away, the residents had been spared her mother's kamikaze approach to driving. After her father's death, people forgave her backing over their mailboxes or going up on the curb and squashing the flowers planted there, because of her grieving state. Most of the police went easy on her, often stopping her, but letting her get by with a friendly warning. They probably thought she was a confused senior citizen, unaware that she'd always have a dangerous lead foot. Instead of getting a ticket as she should, the few deputies that existed in Legacy's younger days probably asked Lead Foot Cecilia to slow down or even referred the matter to her husband.

Donna hadn't really contemplated her death despite seeing its handiwork in the hospital, and she refused to meet it blindly, which explained the open window. On the way back, she'd call a cab or even walk. Her toes wiggled in her sandals, reminding her it would be a long, slow, possibly blister-inducing stroll.

The sidewalks were crowded with clumps of youngish people, many wearing ball caps with logos and most sporting a backpack, looking ready to take off to hike the cliffs. Quite a few of the men had beards which made it hard to gauge their age, but she assumed they were young. Trends tended not to matter to most older males.

A few, however, like Harvey down at the bank, jumped on the trends, thinking it made them look young. By now her friendly bank teller had shaved his head, pierced both ears, had a tattoo sleeve that was partially done because the pain was too much, and a scraggly beard decorating his chin. He'd asked Donna one day if it made him look younger than his forty-five years. Not wanting to hurt his feelings, she agreed, well aware of how he was hoping to attract a female companion. With any luck, he might find a wannabe pirate lady friend at the Columbus Days celebration.

Speak of the devil, a woman in a tri-corner hat waved in Donna's direction. Then again, she might not be waving at her but at someone across the street. There might be hope for Harvey after all. People lined both sides of the street.

As they moved closer to the heart of the city, the car slowed. Cecilia gave up on weaving and settled into tailgating. How in the world had she missed her mother's atrocious driving when she was a child? As a youngster, the high-speed races to the store were fun, not life-threatening.

The car slowed even more as they stopped for a light that even her mother couldn't justify rushing. A Little Bit of Paris' outdoor café tables were filled with tourists enjoying a drink or meal. Legacy was enjoying an economic boom. Summer months increased traffic as word of mouth spread the news that Legacy's beach was as pretty as any of the Outer Bank beaches, but much less crowded.

Parking was tight with every inch of street space taken. A few had even parked their scooters on the sidewalk and two of those tiny cars that looked like they should belong to Shriners or very small clowns were parked at an angle on one spot. She didn't see how her mother would be able to successfully park Simon's new car, considering she had worse parking skills than Donna, if that were even possible.

"Cecilia, why don't you drive up to the convention center and jump out. I'll park the car. It might end up being quite a walk. You can show your daughter and Herman around while I take care of the parking."

Her mother turned her head to reply to Simon, causing the rest of them to shout. "Lookout!"

A woman crossed in front of them with sunglasses and a pot-bellied pig wearing a service animal vest. She continued calmly across the walkway, never flinching, making Donna wonder if she were blind. Better yet, was that the same woman Mark saw the other day? How many guide pigs were out there?

"Put on your emergency lights, put the car in park, and you can get out here." Simon enunciated each word slowly and carefully to not be misunderstood.

Instead of answering, her mother followed instructions, waiting for Simon to round the front of the car and let her out. A car honked behind them as Donna scrambled out of the back seat. A glare at the honker confirmed her initial impression that the honker was not from around there. For locals there were very few reasons to honk, unless your life or some wayward pet's depended on it.

Inside the center, a lighted board told the time and location of each event. A person dressed up as Colonel Mustard from the Clue game was handing out programs. An influx of people had them all moving toward the registration desk.

A jumbled line formed, resembling a many-headed hydra, with many choosing to stand between the lines to better jump into whatever one they thought was moving faster. As they shuffled closer, she heard the registration agent quoting ticket prices and passing out bracelets. Fifty dollars for a day and a hundred for the weekend, just for some games. She could buy some quality spices for that type of money. Donna moved to the left a little to leave the line and make her apologies to the rest of the group. Maybe they could get another sucker to take her place.

Out of the corner of her eye, she spotted the redheaded woman from the inn, along with Giblet and skinny Thor. Another group passed them and called out. It could have been the noise of the crowd, or maybe the other folks had earbuds still plugged into their ears, or it could have been that Donna was one of the few who still had her hearing. Whatever it was, she could catch most of the words.

"Sorry to hear about Loki."

"Joseph was a cool dude."

"Weird."

They shook their heads and moved on as Donna processed what she heard. Loki and Joseph were the same person, which meant Joseph would have led the team to victory. It could have been a long shot, but for some reason, the trio that were arguing mere feet from her were convinced they still had a shot at taking the title. It meant nothing if Ten was right about there being no money prizes. She slid her foot back to maintain her place in line. A couple people behind her grumbled, but she ignored them.

As much as she hated to spend the money to parade around with a scary rabbit head on her body, it might yield vital information. As soon as she could get her bracelet, she needed to catch up with the trio and find out where the tournament was.

When a tired looking registration person greeted her, Donna had an inspired idea.

"Hi. I'm a reviewer. I'm just here to test out the escape puzzle and then write about it. Maybe I could get a discount rate or even free?"

Instead of talking to her, the woman called back over her a shoulder. "We got another one!"

A masculine shout came from an open doorway. "Everyone is a reviewer. Full price."

Donna already had her hand on her wallet, when the employee announced with a noticeable smirk, "You heard the man."

A stream of people entered the building, bypassing the registration area altogether. Obviously, they weren't waiting in line. She gestured to the fast-moving folks, but Herman nudged her before she could point out those who entered without paying.

"Hurry up. I already have my bracelet."

"Ok." She handed her debit card over with some misgivings. Maybe she didn't think the convention would turn Legacy into crime central, but it was hard dealing with mistakes on your debit card with a business that could vanish overnight. Stores, you could notify and threaten not to do future business with them if misused. She took the bracelet and worked her way over to where Herman, Cecilia, and Simon were standing.

Donna did a double take at seeing her mother's sweetie back already. "Simon, I'm surprised to see you back so fast."

He grinned and gestured to the outside. "Got lucky. Someone pulled out just after I dropped you guys off." He glanced at his wrist which sported an expensive wristwatch. "We have about thirty minutes to wander around before our time slot."

Her mother held her hand up as if she was the official guide.

"This way. We can hit the vendor hall first. There might be some board games you might like to pick up for the inn."

Even though the inn already had board games in what she now dubbed the entertainment parlor, most of her younger guests played video games on the big screen. They were occasionally bumped from their place on the couch by their fathers who wanted to catch the game. A few older couples did enjoy a hand of cards or a game of dominoes, but most of the other games were ready for a long sojourn on the island of misfit toys.

What she really wanted to do was find her guests and learn more about the tournament. Cecilia brought up the front while Simon kept company with Donna in the back. Even though she waited to dart after her desired targets, she maintained a conversation with Simon. It would benefit her to know the man better, especially if he ended up being a member of the family. Since Simon was originally from Legacy, no investigation team was needed to research his background. In a world of so many pretenders, Simon Lightwater was the real deal.

In the crowded noisy vendor hall, there were displays for games, books, caricature portraits, and candy shaped in the character of your choice. Shirts, wigs, and costumes were for sale along with secrets to winning various games. Photo opportunities included one where it appeared the person was the toy inside the cardboard package.

Near the macramé booth, she spotted her trio of Sasha, Thor, and Giblet. *Yippee.* Better yet, Ten, along with Sloane and Gwen, were talking to them. Perfect. It would be normal for her to speak to Ten, maybe pass on some news.

"Excuse me," she murmured to Simon before she worked her way around a woman behind a slow-moving double stroller containing two toddlers, both shouting, "I want! I want!" while pointing at almost everything. She was fairly sure they didn't want a macramé plant holder, but she could be wrong.

"Ten!" she shouted, afraid the group might break apart and disappear before she reached them.

Ten half-turned at the sound of her voice. The couple in front of her stopped and grumbled about the lack of dining options. Couldn't they do that and walk? She swerved around them to reach the group. Sloane was talking to the trio about the upcoming tournament. *Bless her.*

Skinny Thor patted his chest as he spoke. "We have as good of a chance of winning the tournament today as we did with Loki as captain. The smaller teams work better."

Giblet's expression of downturned lips and crossed arms didn't offer a similar confidence, while Sasha was more verbal about her feelings. "Fewer team members means the possibility is higher of being put out of the game quicker."

Sounded like losing to Donna, but to be sure she asked Ten, "How do you win the game?"

"If you're playing at home, a good game is a win for everyone. At a tournament, you could be playing for points, which you can get for being victorious in battle, staying alive, and finding treasure. Sometimes, it's a timed tournament, and the team with the most people left is usually the winner. If everyone dies on your team, you're out."

If that was the case, Sasha had a point. "Is there a required number of players and a maximum number?"

"Are you thinking of playing?" Gwen teased, irritating Donna. She'd never really trusted the female after the pretend girlfriend incident that made both Donna and Ten think that she was his girlfriend.

"No, I was just curious."

Her words may have sounded a bit peevish since Gwen held up her hands and took a step back. "Chill."

Maybe she did need to dial it back. She angled her head at Sloane who was in animated discussion with the other three. "What's happening there?"

"They lost two members of their team bringing them down to three. You need four to be in the tournament."

Joseph, she knew about, but there was a second person? With any luck, it wouldn't be someone who died in the proximity of the inn. "Who's the second person?"

Ten's shoulders went up in a shrug. "Some dude that isn't staying at the inn. Guess he's a drive-in attendee. When he heard about Joseph not leading, he dropped out." He glanced both ways before continuing. "Rumor is he joined another team. They're trying to get Sloane to join theirs. She's a good player and has been on other teams. Currently, she's not."

"Do you think she'll play?"

"Yeah. She even told me she wished she'd joined a team, but before the cons were too far away to be affordable."

"Understandable. When does it start?"

"It's on-going. First, they play several elimination games, and then the top teams have a play off." He motioned to the group trying to woo Sloane to their side. "Their game starts at 1:45, give or take a few minutes, since games seldom start or end on time."

They should be done with their escape game by that time. Sure, it was supposed to be an hour, but how hard could it really be? There would be plenty of time to scamper over and watch the tournament.

Ten motioned to the rabbit head. "I see you got stuck with the giant Thumper head."

She cradled the large hare head in her left arm. "Herman is going to be Alice in Wonderland."

"Yeah, that's funny, too." He chuckled. "Maybe not as funny as you trying to figure out anything with that thing on your head."

"What do you mean?" She still held the thought that four mature adults with a vast expanse of practical life experience could figure their way out of any escape room with ease.

Tennyson glanced over at Sloane who was still talking, then reached for the head that Donna surrendered. He popped it on his head and turned fast, causing the head to spin around, then trembled a little before stopping. He pulled it off and handed it back to Donna. "Just as I thought. There's no peripheral vision. You won't be able to see if someone sneaks up on you. All you can do is go forward. Keep your head still to keep it from spinning."

She didn't like the sound of someone trying to startle her intentionally. "Do you think someone will try to scare me?"

"They do in some of the escape rooms. It messes with your thinking."

"Thanks, I think." Just contemplating that someone might jump out tensed up her shoulders. If anyone was foolhardy enough to do that, she'd headbutt them with the rabbit head. It might even destroy it, forcing her to continue the game without the head. The more she considered it, the more she liked the idea.

Sloane joined Ten. "Hey, I'm going to have to go with them and plan our strategy. We don't have much time."

"Okay. You'll miss Donna and the rest of the Alice in Wonderland team in the escape room."

Her top teeth sunk down into her lower lip. "I hate that." Her eyebrows lifted. "Do you think you can film the live feed?"

"Maybe. Depends on if some security guard shoos me away."

Donna didn't want to ask but felt she should. "Live feed?"

"Sure. Parts of the game are displayed on a large screen outside the room. Not all of the game is displayed since it would provide clues on how to escape. Most of what is shown is people looking confused."

"Great." Even though she said the word, it meant anything but great. "There's a reason for this?"

"Yes, and it's hilarious."

Chapter Seventeen

A GROUP OF giggling teenagers dressed in colorful spandex costumes exited the escape room. One of the participants turned slightly and noticed them. "Look who's going next."

The group burst into laughter again. Donna knew what they were thinking. They assumed everything was a physical challenge that their young, fit bodies could handle. Not everything involved speed or muscle, but what if it did? Their combined life experience would count for nothing if they had to sprint anywhere.

The thought of a youth-challenged team—which Donna preferred for a designation as opposed to old fogies-continued to amuse the teens.

"Don't have a heart attack," one advised.

Herman, who normally was a jovial fellow responded. "I'm not your grandpa. If I were, I'd resign my position due to your bad manners."

Instead of hooting even more, the group slunk off, which meant there was some hope for them. Simon was in a deep discussion with the entry person, possibly assuring himself that there would be nothing dangerous inside. If they were smart, though, they'd be careful and possibly settle for mental challenges to avoid lawsuits.

A clipboard with a waiver and pen was passed around for signing. The waiver stated they were not responsible for accidents, psychological trauma, nightmares, or possible heart attack. The other three signed without even fully reading the paper. Did she want to do something that might cause psychological trauma?

She held the pen above the paper as she debated the situation. Finally, her mother shouted, "Come on, Donna! Don't be a baby about this."

"Did you read this?"

Simon shot her a sympathetic look, but her mother was unmoved. "It's the usual legalese. No one really has those issues, but they have to put them out just in case someone decides to sue as a money grab. It's like those disclaimers on the medicine commercials. Sometimes, the disclaimer is longer than the actual commercial."

That didn't help her relax any. She worked in a hospital and did see the side effects from the prescription medicine. It was one of the reasons she avoided the half-dozen prescriptions her own doctor had tried to give her.

She must have looked unconvinced, because Herman nudged her. "Let's show those punk kids that brains beats youth every time."

Not always, but maybe it would this time. The weight of several pairs of eyes made her cave, although her uneasy stomach told her otherwise. She signed with a flourish and handed the clipboard back to the overly made up employee. Was she a zombie? A vampire? A character from a video game that Donna knew nothing about? Maybe her outfit hinted at the adventures within. This was so not going to be fun. Why was she doing this again? Ah yes, *Information.* She was supposed to get information. It looked like Sloane would be her best chance now since she'd be hanging with Joseph's team. Not sure what they would let slip as they played the game, though. Then again, Joseph's death could have been an accident. Donna wanted it to be an accident, an unhappy one, obviously for everyone involved, but mainly Joseph.

Goth/vampire girl launched into her spiel. "You cannot use your cellphones."

A plastic basket was passed around for everyone to deposit their cellphones. For a second, she considered keeping hers. What if they needed to call for help? Herman passed her the basket and cleared his throat. The employee might accept she forgot her phone, but then it chirped. A glance at the screen let her see her undoing was a notice from an app she installed that alerted you whenever you were close to a sale.

"Candyworld is having a bulk sale." She put the phone into the basket.

"Okay." The employee continued. "I don't normally have to say this, but there can be no pencil and paper to work out clues."

Yeah, they probably looked like the pencil and paper type. Her mother opened her purse to prove she had no such items. Good for her. Donna had plenty but put on her clueless face. It must have been a good one because the girl continued, or she really didn't care that much.

"You have sixty minutes in the destroyed lab of Dr. Kildare, who specializes in germ warfare."

The hairs on her arm already stood up. Give her a zombie over germ warfare any day.

"You have five hints." The employee held up her fishnet gloved hand, spreading her fingers apart to represent five. "You can push the call button inside to ask for a hint. After you use your five, there are no more. Don't waste them all at once. There are clues hidden within the room that will lead you to the key. There are also distractions." Her lips tipped up in an evil smile on the last word.

Simon put on his top hat and adjusted his oversized bow tie while her mother put on her queen crown and apron costume. She had her heart scepter in hand and handed the empty bag to the employee. Herman donned his headband without any complaint, which just left her. *Oh, joy.*

She adjusted her cross-the-body purse, then picked up the head. It was big and went over her hair easily and rested on her shoulders. Even though the eyes were large with a mesh screen over them, everything went dark. It reminded her of walking through the house at dusk before she turned on the lights.

"All right participants." Her voice grew louder as she tried to inject some enthusiasm into her tone. "The clock starts now. Good luck, you'll need it."

They shuffled into a room with flickering lights, overturned tables, papers thrown about, and the constant static sound that occurred between radio stations. Simon held up a hand as the door shut behind them with an ominous clang sound effect.

Cecilia spoke before Simon could. "You need to listen to Simon because he researched how to get out of the escape room on his phone."

"Yes, that's right—" Simon started.

"Look everywhere." Her mother interrupted. "Under the carpet. Open cabinets. Turn things over. This isn't someone's house. Be as nosy as you want. I'm counting on you, Donna, since that's your strong skill."

Simon tried to grab back the leadership role again. "Remember, we are a team and depend on each other. No one is on their own."

It was really hard to hear inside the rabbit head. It would probably be even harder to find things. She took off the head to get a good look at her surroundings and to address her mother's nosy remark.

An alarm sounded, and a red light flashed as a voice sounded over the intercom. "Put the rabbit head back on. All participants must remain in full costume. Five minutes has been deducted from your overall time."

Donna put the full mask back on, but she had a bone to pick. "You never said anything about deductions or even keeping the costume on before we came in. That's not fair!"

Her words bounced around inside the papier-maché head, almost deafening her. Her mother asked, "Did you say something, dear?"

Talking would not be one of her options. She moved slowly around the room, trying to focus in the flickering light. Something or someone pushed her, causing a stumble. Her hands broke her fall, but her knees still grazed the floor, bearing witness that it was concrete if anyone wanted to know. Her head tumbled off in the fall, giving Donna a chance to look around for anything she could have tripped over. *Nothing.*

The red alarm sounded again. "That's another five minutes. The rabbit is working against you."

"Donna!" Both Herman and Cecilia shouted her name as she crawled in the direction of her head. Once she found it and put it on, she sat down against the wall. Someone had definitely pushed her. Did anyone ask if she was okay? No. Instead, they yelled because of her costume malfunction.

The sound of dropped items and shutting cabinets meant the others were hard at work. As the only investigator in the group, she should do something. Behind her was a bookshelf filled with books that might contain a clue. The light was dim, and she didn't have her reading glasses, but she did have her lighted magnifying glass in her purse. It would be best if the ogre girl outside didn't see her use it. If she stood, her body would provide a barrier, shielding her actions. Donna pushed up from the floor and surveyed the room for the cameras that were broadcasting their ignoble attempt to be adventurous.

Once she spotted the camera, she angled her body to block its invasive eye. The magnifying glass allowed her to read the titles. Most of the books had scientific sounding titles, but those were only slipcovers for Reader's Digest condensed collections. One of the books felt lighter than the rest and was entitled *The Key to the Universe*. She tried to flip it open, but it wasn't a book at all. It was some type of dummy book or a box designed to look like a book. Using her thumbnail, she located a seam she managed to pry open. Inside the box rested an ornate key and fancy lettering spelling out *You Found It*. She might have a key, but it wasn't any good without a door.

There was no way to communicate with the head on, so she removed it, causing the alarm to shriek, which of course made her the focus of her group. "Where's the door?"

Herman pointed to the door they entered through. The warning announced that they had once again lost five minutes and only had twenty left. Would they exit through the door they entered? Each room might only have one entrance, which meant she might as well try.

She approached the door with her rabbit head in hand and flourished the key.

"You found it?" There was a touch of disbelief in her mother's voice.

Donna chose not to comment on the skepticism and moved the key around the door, looking for a keyhole. She passed it over a black panel that lit up, showing a keyhole and key twisting in it.

A deep sonorous voice announced, "You have freed yourself from the germ warfare lab before you succumbed to the germs."

The door swung open, surprising the attendant who was staring at her phone. The spandex wearing teens had returned and were staring up at the clock that had stopped when the exit unlocked.

The stupid rabbit head, falling, even the annoying alarm was worth it to see the dumbfounded looks on their faces. The one who had warned Herman not to have a heart attack appeared stunned as he mumbled, "They beat our time."

Still a little annoyed at the attendant's failure to tell them about the penalties, Donna spoke. "The rabbit found the key, despite your many attempts to handicap us. That shove was underhanded, but I'm glad you pushed me as opposed to anyone else in my party."

"I didn't push you. No one was in the room with you."

She'd definitely felt hands on her back that had given her a hard shove. It must have been part of the experience. The attendant would deny it, but who else could it have been?

Chapter Eighteen

ERMAN, SIMON, AND Cecilia pranced down the center's wide halls decorated with posters for merchandise, online games, and upcoming events. They were in high spirits after their triumphant exit from the escape room. Donna not so much. She knew it was a fluke. Who knew if they would ever have found the key if she hadn't been stumbling around half blind? It made her wonder how many people passed by that book.

She trailed after the trio as they wove through the crowds. The fact they'd beaten the time of a younger team resulted in bright expressions and smug smiles. Personally, Donna had expected to beat them. Was she not a mystery solver extraordinaire? It usually took no more than sixty minutes for her to unravel a crime unless it was a television show. Those she always had before the third commercial break.

Why hadn't she solved Joseph's rapid departure from this earthly plane though? Herman would be quick to point out there was no viable weapon, motivation, or even a suspect. Had her love of the mystery genre cause her to cry murder where none existed? Did she want to solve this alleged crime to prove she was more than capable to Billings, who had disparaged her skills with his tacky jabs at Mark?

There was some discussion about lunch, which she wasn't opposed to, just nothing that was passed through a food truck window.

She'd heard there were some wonderful chefs in the big city scene working out of food trucks, but she was certain they were not parked out in front of the center.

"We could always go to Janice's restaurant." Her best friend owned a seafood restaurant right on the coast. "With most of the crowd in town, her restaurant might welcome some customers."

Her mother was quick to respond to the suggestion which was probably directly related to her hunger level. "You're right. Let's head out."

As the unofficial leader, Cecilia swerved to the right and headed for an exit. Even though Donna had made the suggestion, she hadn't mean *right now*. A digital wall clock glowed 2:15, making whenever they arrived a late lunch. The group might not be pleased to take a side trip to the tournament room.

"Hey, Uncle Herman." A shout cut through the drone of numerous folks and automated demonstration videos in the various booths. Gwen waved from her position beside Ten on the other side of the hall.

Even though Donna tried to persuade herself into liking Gwen for Herman's sake, it was hard. Why was Ten walking around the center instead of watching his girlfriend battle it out in the tournament? Maybe it was as much fun as watching someone play golf, which was not very. The two crossed over to where they were.

"Why aren't you watching the tournament?"

Gwen cut her eyes to Ten. "One of us got kicked out."

"Hey!" Ten grimaced, wrinkling his nose. "How was I supposed to know that whistling and yelling, 'Way to go,' wasn't appropriate?"

"The gamemaster told us it wasn't conducive for those engaged in serious strategy." Gwen delivered the words in a no-nonsense tone, which had to be a mimic of how they were originally spoken.

"Yeah," Ten shrugged his shoulders. "Gotta hang out until Sloane is finished. What are ya'all doing?"

Herman made a fist and smacked it into his hand. "We beat those punk kids, that's what we did."

"Technically, we beat their time, not them." The way her former neighbor said it, people might think they engaged in a fist fight.

"Good for you, Uncle."

Ten lifted his eyebrows. "What was your strategy?"

As far as Donna could tell they had none.

"We looked everywhere just as Simon said," Cecilia added swinging her wand around to point to Simon but ended up smacking him in the back.

"Ouch!"

"Sorry, sweetie. I'm putting the wand back into the bag. It's time for me to stop being the queen before someone else gets hurt."

Donna's lips twitched at suppressing her laughter, but she could control it. Herman apparently couldn't.

"That was a hoot!" He managed to pull his laughter back to a few gasps, then asked, "Are you okay?"

"Fine," Simon assured them. "The game of love is never easy."

The remark had Cecilia patting Simon's arm at his public declaration. It made Donna breathe a little easier. Her mother had finally found someone closer to her age who treated her well. Her mother's flirtation with dating younger men had been awkward, at least for Donna. She'd lived with the fear she might end up with a stepfather who was her own age.

"Donna!" Mark's voice rang out over the crowd.

He stood near the vendor hall main entrance and waved both arms to get their attention. Good heavens, they didn't have him taking tickets or checking bracelets? She scurried over to her husband. "What is it?"

"Maria has been trying to call you. She needs to take Cici home, something about her running a temp."

"Oh, that's too bad. Fairly normal for babies depending on how high the temp is. Why didn't she just call me?" Her mouth dropped open as she remembered. "We forgot our phones!" Their victory march hadn't included stopping for phones. "We've got to go get them."

She'd already pivoted and was headed out with Simon and Cecilia trailing when she noticed Herman missing. "Should we wait?"

"No," Cecilia pointed to her beau. "Herman told Simon to get his phone if the attendant will allow it. He wanted to talk to Mark about finally getting the box home and opened. You know, the one you never mentioned to me."

Her mother sounded a trifle miffed, but not overly so. "It's not like we told everyone. The plan was to keep it quiet to cut down on the trespassers. You know how it goes. If one box is found people assume there will be more. I'd have people burrowing under the inn like gophers."

"Was there anything interesting in the box?"

"Probably not, but so far no one has opened it."

"Mercy. Why not?"

"Time. There never seems to be enough of it with the Con, the bone crew, and the ridiculous schedule Mark has been working. He put the box in his trunk and has been driving it around. The forensic anthropologist wants the box opened, thinking it might help date the skeleton. Whatever is in the box would have been buried at the same time as the mysterious woman who became our skeleton."

They had basically race-walked back to the escape room where bystanders huddled around the live monitors. Donna pretended to watch the monitor as she got her breath back. A group of red-uniformed folks who were smart enough not to wear masks stood inside the escape room discussing what they should do. Their comments were broadcasted to the people in the hall, which made Donna cringe. What had she said? No worries. None of it would have been worthy of being repeated. No one would have been able to understand her, anyhow.

One of the participants murmured about needing to go to the bathroom. Ms. Siren Happy got on the microphone. "Not an option. You have forty minutes left."

Donna inched her way up to the stand and waited for when the female wasn't staring at the screen and devising new ways to torment the participants.

The woman finally looked away from the screen. "Oh, it's you, Rabbit Head."

"Actually, it's Donna. We came back for our phones."

The plastic basket was produced, allowing them to pick out their phones without any supervision. As they strolled back to Mark and Herman, she marveled at what had just happened. "She never even looked at what phones we were taking."

Cecilia patted her chest. "That's because we look trustworthy."

"Nice thought," Simon said, "but I think it was more that she didn't care."

There was another reason to like Simon as opposed to her mother's previous beaus. The man told it as it was. No sugar-coating things and putting all positive spins on stuff, except when it came to Cecilia. That, she'd put down to love. Only a truly smitten man could have suffered the harrowing ride into town without cursing.

By the time they arrived Herman was in an animated discussion with Mark. "Why couldn't our female skeleton be a jewel thief?"

Mark asked, the twinkle in her sweetie's eye meaning he wasn't backing down.

Apparently, Herman wasn't either and retorted, "I know women nowadays want to do everything that men do, but that wasn't the case a hundred years ago. Women didn't commit crimes."

A couple passing by felt the need to comment. "Are you kidding me? What planet are you living on?"

Her former neighbor's face flushed as his shoulders stiffened. Maybe they all had underestimated just how invested Herman was in the tale. Her fingers touched his arm as she spoke. "We need to go now if you want lunch. Simon will have to drop me off at the inn, but you can bring me back some gumbo and Johnny bread."

They made their goodbyes all around. Ten promised to head back as soon as Sloane finished the tournament.

"Make sure you invite Sloane to supper." It would be hard to pick her brain without her there.

"Sure. What are you making?"

"What do you think she'd like?"

"Chicken enchiladas." He gave an emphatic head bob.

No need to mention it happened to be one of Ten's favorite dishes, but it didn't mean Sloane wouldn't like it, too. With everyone there, including the bone crew, she'd have to triple the recipe. Normally, it would take thirty minutes to fix, but more food required a longer prep time, especially since she'd have to bake the chicken.

"See you later, sweetie." Donna wanted to at least give Mark a peck on the cheek, but as soon as she did Billings would appear like an evil genie in a puff of smoke. Maybe she was guilty of overdramatizing the commissioner, but he did seem to lurk around worse than a dark cloud.

In the car, she couldn't resist teasing Herman about the skeleton. "Why don't you like the idea of a female crook?"

"It just wasn't done back then," he muttered and folded his arms as if the end of the subject.

"Why not? If people didn't suspect women of being capable of a crime, they wouldn't be watched. Plenty of women were spies during the Civil War. The joke was on the men who casually allowed them to go through enemy lines believing they were just confused, empty-headed women."

Cecilia turned in the passenger seat to join the conversation. "I even heard Jefferson Davis had a slave in his home who regularly read his mail and listened in to his meetings. His assumption was that slaves couldn't read and write. Many could, despite there being a law against educating them."

"War is different." Herman's arms stayed folded, and his chin went up a little. "Why would a woman steal jewels? It was obviously a risky venture. Security was more likely to shoot and ask questions later."

"Money," Cecilia answered abruptly. "Isn't that the reason anyone ever steals?"

That was the assumption most people made. "People steal for a variety of reasons. Someone who wants to get back at someone steals for revenge, taking something that matters. A theft could be a matter of pride to show off. Other times, a person is coerced into stealing to prove something."

"Such as?" Cecilia inquired as she straightened in her seat.

"I'm not talking about myself. I'm sure gangs have rituals where members have to mug someone. Teenagers sometimes dare each other to shoplift. As for our skeleton, she had a possible engagement ring on her hand. Her fiancé could have been a jewel thief who wooed her only because of her possible proximity to the jewels. After the robbery, they may have argued. It could have been his intention the entire time to get rid of her after she proved her love to him by stealing."

"Hmm." Herman's arms loosened, and his hands dropped into his lap. He relaxed back in his seat with a long exhale. "I didn't want to believe a woman was involved in the jewel heist, but you make a convincing argument. I wonder if the male thief, shocked by what he had done, buried the jewels next to the murdered woman and was shot leaving, since there *was* a body of a known thief found in Legacy."

That would tie things up nicely. Unfortunately, life bore no resemblance to a crime show, but recently there had been a few that were open-ended allowing the criminals to get away. "Don't know. There could have been a third person who killed both of them. I guess it all depends on what's in the box."

Simon, who had been silently and efficiently driving, decided to comment. "Will the forensic anthropologist be able to tell if the woman was murdered?"

"Maybe. Depends on how it happened. A bashed in skull would be obvious, but I've seen the skull, and it's whole. If she was stabbed and the murderer took the knife with him, we'd never know. While they have the majority of the bones, they don't have all of them."

It all boiled down to what was in the box. If there weren't jewels, it ruined all their scenarios based on jewel thieves.

Chapter Nineteen

W HEN SIMON PULLED into the parking lot, she couldn't help but notice the bright work lights directed underneath the house. There were a couple of pairs of feet sticking out from under the house. It looked like someone had dropped the inn on them like the wicked witch in *The Wizard of Oz* movie. As she drew closer, one of the feet moved backward, revealing bare calves, then thighs, and a swath of denim that might be mistakenly labeled shorts.

"Dr. Haddox, I found it."

The rest of Elle wiggled out from under the inn, holding a screen box with a tiny strip of vertebrae. Curious about what she found, Donna moved closer. The second pair of feet did the backward wiggle out from under the house. Dr. Haddox, clay streaks all over her clothes, managed to maintain her haughty superiority and gave Donna a cool look of acknowledgment. Not to be outdone, Donna merely lifted her eyebrows in response.

It didn't stop Donna from moving in closer to peer in the screen box, almost bumping heads with Dr. Haddox in the process. It was her skeleton, and those neck bones were hers, too. Her finger went out, brushing the bones and turning them over. The outraged gasp of Dr. Haddox didn't deter her at all.

"The hyoid bone is broken," Donna mused aloud. "It sometimes happens during strangulation."

She removed her hand and stepped back, aware that Dr. Haddox was anxious to check out the find on her own. Her elegant fingers clad in latex carefully examined the bones, then met Donna's eyes.

"I concur, which explains why she was buried where she was."

The theory her mother and she concocted in the car might be closer to the truth than she originally thought. Now, all that was needed was to open the box to square things away.

"We will probably never know who she was if she wasn't local." The thought caused a pang that some lovesick girl threw her life away on someone so unworthy. "I imagine we can still bury her in a proper cemetery."

"Are you sure about that?" Dr. Haddox cocked her head in that superior manner she had. It looked like their momentary truce was over.

"I'm not exactly sure what the law is. Mark will know. I can bet it isn't throw the bones away in the trash." Donna rubbed the clay dust on her pants. "I assume all the bones have been found."

"They have." The chill wafted off Dr. Haddox in waves, despite it being ninety with close to eighty on the humidity scale.

"Good. I imagine ya'all will want to pack up. I'm fixing chicken enchiladas tonight, and we can open a bottle of bubbly if you want to celebrate." Donna would be celebrating the return of the elevator crew and the opportunity to sleep in her own bed.

Dr. Haddox carried the screen tray with the vertebrae in it as if it were a sacrificial offering and she the high priestess. She slipped past Donna, answering in a clipped tone. "That would be acceptable."

Don't show too much enthusiasm. It might be too much for you. She would have assumed the bone folks would be happy to return to their homes. Sometimes there was no figuring out folks. There were chickens that needed defrosting.

Elle sprinted and joined her as she entered via the back door.

"Donna, could I talk to you?"

"Sure." She couldn't imagine what the child wanted unless it was more towels or possibly the name of a local store that sold decent clothes. Inside the kitchen, she pulled out two organically raised chickens she'd have to defrost one at a time.

"Why is the skeleton important to you?"

Good question. It made her think as she prepped the first chicken for defrosting. "The way I see it is this woman had a short life and not necessarily a happy one. Someone should grieve for her, acknowledge her, then honor her with a proper burial. Heaven forbid that you should drop dead today and decades later your bones are found in some marsh. How would you like to be treated?"

Elle sighed and leaned against the counter. "You make it hard."

The girl was making no sense. "How so?"

"I was supposed to come in here and argue for the right for us to take the bones back to the university and put them on display or use them in the program. It's obvious I won't sway you from your bones."

Donna pulled out the cookbook, turned to the recipe, and laid the book down, open to the page. "When you get right down to it, none of us have rights to her skeleton. It would be a different story if she left her body to science, which she didn't. I have a feeling she might not be too fond of people taking photos of what's left of her."

"You've got a point. Kelvin tells me that box you haven't opened is full of jewels. Is it?"

So much for keeping things quiet. "How does he know?"

"I think some kid in the neighborhood told him. Apparently, some old man has been telling that tale for years."

Yeah, she knew exactly who the old man was. "Tell him not to get his hopes up." I've done my best to not anticipate something that might not happen."

"Okay, I will. If Dr. Haddox asks, could you say I made a persuasive argument?"

"Will do." Wherever Dr. Haddox was, Elle was, which made her wonder about the other assistant who was nowhere to be found. "What happened to Kelvin?"

Elle shrugged and sneered with her eyes, which she must have picked up from Dr. Haddox. "The heat was too much for him. He needed to rest."

It sounded more like he needed to loaf, making Donna wonder why the man was pursuing a career he had no real interest in. "I guess I'll see him at supper."

"No doubt." Elle pushed through the kitchen door and into the foyer.

Good gracious! Had everyone been parading through her kitchen? "Maria. Maria!"

Her sister-in-law strolled into the kitchen with the baby on one hip. "I heard you the first time."

"How's Cici?" She bent to press her lips against the dark hair, feeling her temperature. "She seems fine."

"Oh, she is."

"What about the call?"

"Oh, that. I just wanted someone back here, because that hot dog dude came back, which surprised me. I thought he should be at the convention selling everyone overpriced wieners, possibly on stale buns. Then he starts this creepy stuff about am I all alone here?"

"Weird."

"I started carrying Cici around since nothing wards off men like a crying baby."

"Did Cici oblige?"

Her sister-in-law tossed back a handful of her dark hair. "I wish. I guess she enjoyed being carried around. She was angelic, all smiles and coos. I even poked Jasper with my foot to get him up, but all he did was sleep."

On hearing his name, the puggle raised his head and gave a single bark. Maria threw him a disgusted glance. "Too late now. I called everyone and the only person who answered was Mark. The dude was standing right there so I couldn't say anything about him. It would have tickled him pink to know he had me rattled. I wasn't giving him that pleasure. He's gone now. Odd, that Kelvin guy went with him."

Donna couldn't remember if she'd seen the two men had ever talk to each other, but since she wasn't there at night, they could have struck up an acquaintanceship without her knowing. Normally, a friendship was a good thing. Call it woman's intuition or instinct, but she felt nothing good could come up from this pairing.

"Sorry you had to deal with that."

Maria closed her eyes for a moment before saying, "It's odd. Normally, I'd show someone like him the door. Besides it being your inn and that would so not be good for business, I felt real fear like I never have before. I couldn't let anything happen to Cici."

Lord have mercy! She was bopping around with a rabbit head on while Maria was trying to deal with Mr. Creepy. She wrapped Maria in a loose embrace. "Can you forgive me for not having my phone on?"

"Yes. Daniel didn't answer, either, but he might have to work a little harder to make it up to me."

Donna gave her sister-in-law an extra squeeze before letting go. "I'm here now. Making chicken enchiladas if you want to stay. Did I ever tell you Mom and I were afraid Daniel might screw things up with you?"

"No. Why did you think that?"

"He'd never bring you around. We had to hear about you from other people. At first, I thought you'd be insulted, then I realized he thought either I or Cecilia would say something. What could we possibly say that would upset you?"

"Your mom did tell me she appreciated that I wore more clothing than his previous girlfriend."

Donna chuckled. "That was a compliment. I hope you realized that."

"I decided to take it as one. We're going to go. I need a bath. I feel so slimy dealing with that jerk. I feel sorry for you."

The first chicken was defrosted. She slid the second one into the microwave. Another microwave would help out in times like these. Normally, if she knew what she was making she could thaw it in the fridge but since she needed an excuse to have Sloane over, it was the microwave.

"Don't feel sorry for me. The man will be gone tomorrow. We'll never see him again and will think about him less. You girls go make the best of the rest of your day. I'd hug you goodbye, but I now have raw chicken hands."

Maria blew her a kiss and picked up the diaper bag. "I knew I'd get someone to come to the inn. I was kinda hoping it would be you since you tend not to take any crap off from anyone."

The image of her kicking out Mr. Creepy made her smile. She wouldn't do it unless he did something really bad, and secretly she was hoping he would. "I need to protect my rep and not go all soft on you."

"Not worried. See ya."

"Let me walk you to your car. I'd offer to hold Cici, but—"

"Yeah, I know. Raw chicken hands."

Donna turned to push open the door with her hip as opposed to her hands, not wanting to smear the handles. It would have taken only a few seconds, but she felt the need to assure herself that Maria and Cici got off safely. She stood in the parking lot waving as they exited.

Elle was picking up equipment and carrying it to the university van. The slender girl struggled with the extra-long folding table. Donna in good conscience could not leave the girl to struggle with the stubborn table. As much as she hated doing it she rubbed her hands on her pants. She'd have to wash them in hot water now.

"Here, let me help." She hurried over to where Elle wrestled with the table. The two of them got it folded and stowed in the van. "Do you have anything else?"

"There are a couple of tool boxes in the inn, but we'll load them tomorrow." She clenched her hands into fists. "Kelvin should do something instead of napping all day."

"Oh, he's not napping." Donna didn't see any reason to protect the man who didn't strike her as very industrious.

"What do you mean?" Elle's fisted hands found purchase on her hips.

Bless her heart. The girl was about as ferocious as a puppy. "He took off to town with the hot dog vendor guy."

"That jerk!" Her lips pressed together, and her eyes narrowed. "He's been worse than useless. The only reason Dr. Haddox included him is that she thought he'd be good at hauling things around. You saw how that worked out."

Donna settled for nodding since the sight of an enraged Elle made her want to smile.

"I think I need to talk to Dr. Haddox."

Not trusting herself to speak, Donna watched Elle march across the yard. In a few years, she'd probably have her own assistants to fetch and carry. Donna was willing to bet the woman wouldn't ever take on anyone like Kelvin, at least knowingly.

Chapter Twenty

THE ENCHILADAS WERE in the oven baking when Donna looked out the kitchen window and spotted the hot dog truck. *Really?* He must have given up early on the convention crowd, or the participants were more selective than she gave them credit. She hadn't heard the food truck pull up, but it could have happened when some of the other guests returned, filling the foyer with laughter and chatter.

Mark's voice carried as he guided a small statured man with slightly out of control gray curls reminiscent of Einstein up the front porch stairs. Tucked under Mark's arm was the box that incited so much curiosity. At last, she'd see if they would be putting a pool in the backyard or not.

"Donna, we have company."

She whipped her apron over her head and checked her hair in the reflective door of the microwave before exiting the kitchen. "Hello."

Up close the man looked vaguely familiar, but she couldn't place him.

He grasped her outstretched hand and gave it a good shake. "It's good to see you. It's been many years since you accompanied your father to my store to pick out your mother's present."

He was the jeweler. It all came rushing back. At the time, his hair was brown, not gray, and he seemed taller, probably because she wasn't then. Donna enjoyed the trips, feeling like she was part of the process of picking out something special for her mother. When she entered her teen years, she discovered her mother pre-shopped, and Mr. Jensen had a list of everything that would be an acceptable gift.

"It's so nice to see you. It *has* been years. Are you still running the store?"

"It's my son's now. He took over probably twenty years ago, but since he assumed the position I have been able to pursue some of my pastime interests."

She assumed it would be golf or raising rare orchids. "What are those?"

"I make paste jewelry. Very fine paste jewelry. Only experts like myself can tell." He drew back his shoulders and pushed out his chest with pride.

Mark added, "He makes replicas of expensive, famous jewels for people all around the world. He's even done some for royalty."

"How nice for you." What she really wanted to know was what did it have to do with her. Maybe Mark had been friends with the man for a while. "Have you and Mark been friends long?"

"I've known of him. Who hasn't heard of the helpful Detective Taber? I'd say we have become better acquainted recently. I bet you're anxious to see what's in the box."

At last, they were getting to it. "We could go into the parlor." She had almost said the dining room but remembered just in time there might be a skeleton still spread out on the blue tarp. "There's a nice round table in there we can use."

Mark placed the box on the table and winked at her. "I think you're going to be surprised."

There was the snick of a gun cocking and an oily voice said, "Not as surprised as you're going to be. Put your gun on the ground."

Mark moved slowly, turning as he placed his gun on the carpet. Donna turned her head only to find Kelvin had a gun trained on her as hot dog guy reached for Mark's gun. Were they just going to allow this to happen? Her eyes must have telegraphed the question because her husband's lips moved forming the word, *No*.

Mr. Creepy reached for the box and grinned. "Would you like a little peek at what you won't have?"

He found the latch and opened the box, which must have been pried open earlier for it to open so easily. Inside the case were velvet bags. Kelvin yelled from the side, "Is that what I think it is?"

"Just what I promised you." The top of the bag loosened enough to display the shine and fire of jewels. Some as small as a dime and a few as large as quarters. He tossed them back into the box. "My goal was to relieve you of your goodies in the middle of the night, which would leave you with a house full of suspects. I couldn't take a chance you might decide to take your newfound treasures to the bank."

There was the sound of car doors slamming. More guests returning. This could turn into a bloodbath. Jasper erupted into a barking frenzy and charged out of the kitchen. Not knowing what the dog would do, the men tried to keep an eye on the dog and Mark at the same time. Mark used the distraction to heave the heavy table over, scattering the jewel bags. One fell open spilling its glittering treasures.

Hot dog guy lunged for the jewels while Kelvin shouted, "What should we do now?"

Donna dropped to the floor in case bullets started flying and realized she was at the perfect level to grab the oriental runner and pull. Before she could do anything, Ten crept out of the kitchen brandishing a cast iron skillet.

Skillets could be handy but were no match for guns. She'd have to keep the man's attention focused on her. "Are you giving up your forensic anthropology career for a life of crime?"

Kelvin gave a derisive snort and waved the gun in Donna's directions. "I was going to give it up, anyhow. Who wants to spend their time picking through trash and dirt to piece together a body? It's a poor excuse for a career. I lucked out when I bumped into a money-making opportunity drinking in the television room. As for more crimes, this one job should do me."

The tremor in his hand denied his tough words. He might end up shooting wildly, injuring or killing almost everyone in the room. Mark was fighting his own battle as he traded punches with the vendor who was unfortunately younger and stronger than him. Mr. Jensen stood pressed back against the wall clutching the bottle of wine he'd brought.

Someone yelled, "Watch out!" which propelled Donna to the floor with her cheek against the floor, the oriental rug chafing her face, and the whizz of a bullet hurtled over her head. From her angle, she saw Mr. Jensen's legs dart in Mark's direction. With a, "Take that!" A thump of a body hitting the floor followed.

Was Mark okay? She pushed up to see Kelvin clutching his arm and blood seeping through his fingers. Had he shot himself or was he the victim of a double cross?

Ten, sensing his opportunity, darted in and crowned the wounded man, sending him to his knees.

As she moved to a crouching position to check out Mark's situation, she saw Dr. Haddox in the hall with a snub-nosed pistol. It looked like the inn needed a metal detector for guests if they all were packing. The blonde had a grim line to her mouth, making Donna uncertain if she was one of the good guys until she pointed to Kelvin with her pistol.

"No one makes fun of forensic science." Her accent thickened probably due to anger and stress. "I never wanted you on my team to begin with. Your father-in-law, the chancellor, made me take you, passing over good candidates."

If Donna hadn't been a fan of Rocky and Bullwinkle cartoons with appearances by Russian spies Boris and Natasha, she might not have been able to understand the woman, but she would have recognized the look in her eyes, which was disgust.

The sound of fighting on the other side of the room had stopped. Mark had Mr. Creepy on his stomach and his hands pulled up behind him as he snapped on the cuffs. Mr. Jensen loomed over the two loosely holding the bottle in his right hand.

The kitchen door opened as Sloane and Gwen rushed out, clutching Donna's new chef knife and a can of aerosol olive oil. The latter would just make people greasy. The sound of clapping startled Donna enough to stand. She stepped over the prone Kelvin to look out in the hall where some of her guests stood.

Giblet waved at her and queried, "Why didn't you tell anyone you were going to do a live-action role play? We missed most of it."

The thought of them parading in while fists and bullets were flying made her lean against the wall for support. She closed her eyes briefly as she tried to think of a proper response, but Gwen's voice rang out, startling Donna.

"It was just a rehearsal. We aren't ready for the public, yet. We'd appreciate it if you'd go back to your rooms, now. We'll call you when we're ready."

Donna opened her eyes to see the guests making their way to their rooms. Gwen's quick thinking had just bought her time. She wasn't totally sure what she'd do when the guests asked about the role play later though. Maybe she could tell them they just weren't good enough.

Her feet made an unsteady path to where Dr. Haddox stood in the hall. She pocketed her gun and shrugged. "I must always be prepared on location. You never know."

Even though it pained her to say it, Donna knew it needed to be said. "Thank you. You may have saved my life, possibly all our lives."

A slow smile brightened her face. "Your thanks are accepted. Kelvin would be more likely to shoot himself." She glanced in the direction of her downed assistant. "Still, uncertain people can be like a time bomb." She pointed back at herself. "Your thanks are well earned."

A siren sounded in the distance, which meant Mark had made the call. A buzzer came from the kitchen drawing her attention. The chicken enchiladas were done. After all the excitement, a good meal would be welcome.

THE SKELETON, WHOM Dr. Haddox had named Julia, had been relocated to Ten's room to keep her out of the public view. Ten and Sloane carried in the chips and salsa while Mark wrestled with opening the wine. Kelvin's absence allowed Cecilia to take his seat while Simon pulled up a chair close beside her. Herman, upset over missing out on the excitement, insisted on details.

Details would be nice. The fact that Mr. Jensen had used a broom to round up the jewels had stunned her. Mark kept telling her they weren't real, which she'd suspected. Let's face it. Falling into an unexpected windfall just didn't happen to her. Other people, maybe.

Mark poured champagne into the flutes and passed them out.

Once seated, he started his tale. "I've listened to Herman's tales many times and have considered the unlikelihood of someone allowing their jewels to go out on tour. From my research on jewel thieves, I discovered most heists are from safes where the jewels are kept. Even those who own the spectacular jewels seldom wear them in public, knowing they could be stolen. Instead, they have fake copies made."

He nodded at Mr. Jensen, who had his flute up to his mouth. He put down the glass and cleared his throat. "Even while I was a jeweler, I was in the business of selling fake or enhanced jewels to people who could not afford the real thing. I studied how to make paste jewels as they are called, although today, the paste part is usually made with computers and 3-D printers that can make amazing copies. It would take a jeweler well versed in copies to tell the difference. The fact that these copies are being placed in real gold or platinum settings does make them somewhat valuable and harder to discern."

Donna portioned out the enchiladas and passed the plates around. She could tell Mr. Jensen was just getting warmed up to his subject. As she recalled he could talk about jewelry indefinitely and asked, "When did Mark enter the picture?"

"Yesterday. He contacted me and brought the box by. Getting that open made me feel like a safecracker." He gave a little laugh. "In the end, Mark took a chisel to it."

Dr. Haddox held up a finger. "Was there anything that would indicate a date?"

"Yes," Mark answered instead of Jensen, "There was a flyer about the exhibition. It had the name of the Lowery Diamonds exhibition and the day, but not the year. According to the Internet, the jewels were stolen in 1910 while on tour. I took a picture of the flyer since everything went downtown to the evidence locker."

Not everything. Donna's hand dipped into her pocket and fingered the two stones she picked up from the carpet. Nice looking gems, obviously not perfect, but she was sure Herman would appreciate having one.

Dr. Haddox murmured her appreciation while Herman waved his fork for attention. Thankfully, there was no food on it.

"Okay. The jewels were paste. I'm sure the family had them insured. I remember reading about that in the clippings my father kept. What happened to the real jewels?"

Mark and Mr. Jensen exchanged glances. At Jensen's nod, Mark spoke. "Several things could have happened. Since the fake jewels were on tour, they could have kept the real ones at home. The actual jewelry could have been taken apart and the diamonds sold over the years. It wasn't unusual for wealthy families to discreetly sell off their assets. They could have taken the insurance payout with the intention of having the," he stopped to make air quote marks, "jewels" he closed the quotes, "stolen."

This brought them to their skeleton, which was the part that intrigued her after finding out she wasn't a millionaire. "Do you think the actual robbery was planned by the owners?"

Mark picked up his flute, took a sip, then steepled his fingers. "While the theft was good, bypassing all the security, the fallout, which included two possible dead bodies, the skeleton, and the bullet-riddled jewel thief found the next day, indicates something was put together at the last minute. Consider the jewels remained in the foundation for over a century. If there was a third person, he, or possibly she, had no clue what happened to the jewels."

Mark stopped talking to enjoy his meal.

Mr. Jensen jumped in. "Even though I could tell the jewels were paste almost immediately, most would not be able to." He nodded in Donna's direction. "I doubt the thieves ever knew they had paste jewelry and it makes me wonder how hard the family worked to get their jewels back. Did they just go through the motions just so no one would realize they weren't real to begin with?" He shrugged his shoulders, having no answer.

The conversation drifted to other things after the diamonds eventually were worn out as conversation fodder. Mark's phone chimed, bringing Donna's head up. She'd talk to him later about having the phone at the table. Due to the man technically being on call, she agreed it would be acceptable to not see the phone during meals. Still, he pulled it out and read whatever text was there, then snorted.

"What is it?"

He took a look around the table, judging if he should say anything before speaking. "The hot dog vendor had a long criminal history."

"No surprise there. Maria commented on how he gave off a slimy vibe."

Mr. Jensen had a forkful of enchilada almost to this mouth but put it down to speak. "Many jewel thieves can be quite charming and convincing. They have to be to insert themselves into the homes of the super wealthy."

The one thing she'd never be was super wealthy, but all this talk of diamonds did inspire a perfect surprise trip for Mark. One he'd never see coming despite how well he knew her.

Chapter Twenty-One

O N THE LAST official day for Gen Con some of the attendees had already left. They had jobs and lives that could only be put on hold for so long. They'd packed up their T-shirts that made game references that only other gamers understood. Her guests, due to checkout time being noon, were gone. Herman and Gwen had left earlier. Her old neighbor didn't have too much to say on his way out.

Since the convention didn't turn out to be the chaos the police commissioner expected, Mark had the day off for a change. They were doing a slow walk-through, checking for damage or any missing items in the public rooms. The wear and tear of daily use hadn't figured into her inn budget, so she tried to do any repairs only when needed and for as cheap as possible. The free for all in the front parlor hadn't helped.

Mark held up a throw pillow that had a brown stain on it. "I guess this is one for the dumpster."

Even though it was barely a yard of material and foam form, throw pillows could be surprisingly expensive. She reached for the pillow. "I think not." She held it up and sniffed it. "Coffee. I can get that out."

"I can't believe you just sniffed a pillow," Mark teased, but before she could say anything, the bell on the front door jingled as it opened.

Donna still held the throw pillow as she turned to see who it was. The slender frame of their recent guest filled the doorway. That was odd. Mark was the first to react. It was the polite young man who had helped her with the lemonade that one day. Donna remembered the overheard conversation where he insisted on being called Thor. If ever a name did *not* fit, it was that one since the awkward man was far from being the God of Thunder. Sloane had told them how whiny he was in the tournament, especially after dying with an unfortunate roll of the dice.

Mark nodded in acknowledgment. "Hi, Henry. Did you forget something?"

The man lingered in the doorway, neither entering or backing up. She might not know what he wanted, but she did know he was letting the air conditioning out. It was hard enough to keep the temps at optimum levels with the construction work in the hallway.

"Come on in. Tell us what you need."

He shuffled into the parlor and plopped into a wing chair with a heavy sigh. "I'm not cut out for this."

Here she thought Mark was the king of cryptic phrases. It must be a reference to the convention. She shot Mark a look. He shrugged in response. Apparently, he had no more clue than she did.

"Well," she started, not sure of what to say. "Henry," using a person's name was also an excellent stalling technique. "This is the last day of the Con. You can go home and relax."

He shook his head slowly. His nostrils flared as he took a deep breath and rocked into a ramrod posture in the chair. The boy was steeling himself for something.

Mark must have interpreted his actions, too. "Do you have something you need to say?"

It amazed Donna how Mark managed to convey warmth and

interest in his questions.

Henry nodded but didn't say anything.

This was a puzzle. If there was something they needed to know such as he broke something in his room or took all the snacks in the pantry, an email would have served. Most didn't even do that.

Finally, Henry shifted to the edge of the chair, then glanced up at Mark briefly before he spoke. "I came back here because," he pointed to Mark, "you seem reasonable and kind. Remember we spoke at the Con while you were standing watch."

"It wasn't exactly standing watch. More of a police presence."

It was tough stifling her need to add she, also, was both kind and reasonable, but interrupting Henry would only delay what he had to say. At the rate things were going, it would be a while. She took a seat on the chair facing Henry.

Mark's lips lifted up into a practiced smile. "Go on. What do you have to tell me?"

"My friend, Joseph Carpenter, is dead."

That wasn't news to any of them.

"Yes." Mark spoke only one word holding to his theory that the less someone talked the more likely the other person would.

There were beds upstairs that needed to be stripped. She thought of rocking to her feet to finish her errands, but curiosity kept her firmly in place. What forced this earnest young man to return to the inn?

"Joseph and I have been friends since high school. I met him when he joined a local Dungeons and Dragons group at our library. My mother thought the group would be a good way for me to make friends." His lips tipped up into a sad smile. "You'd be surprised how competitive the players can be."

Mark said nothing, but merely lifted his brows, which appeared to be enough. Henry resumed his narrative. Obviously, he needed to talk about the death of his friend. She leaned back in her chair, expecting a long recital of things he had done with Joseph.

"I guess I was drawn to Joseph because he was such a horrible player. I considered myself a good player at the time and felt protective toward him. Not only was he the worst player in the group, but the scrawniest, too. It's always the littlest ones who get picked on."

Jerks! If there were any way for Donna to reach back in time and give those bullies a good talking to, she would. Her only hope was that karma would catch up with them at some point. She found herself pulled into the beginnings of Joseph and Henry's relationship. "Did he ever become a better player?"

Mark shot her a look that reminded her he happened to be the law authority in the room, but so far it didn't seem to her that his expertise was especially needed. What Henry needed was a comforting shoulder to cry on. Come to think of it, that did sound a lot more like Mark. She'd be more likely to spout some truism like time heals all wounds due to being uncomfortable with his excessive emotional display.

Henry nodded. His hands moved over one another as if he were washing them, sans water, of course. The fact he hadn't looked at his hands meant he was unaware of his body language. His restless hands conveyed nervousness. What did he have to be nervous about?

The iconic light bulb glowed over her head as she put the pieces together. Thank goodness she had her phone in her pocket. She withdrew it and pretended to look at a text message while turning on the recorder app she'd downloaded for just such a purpose. Previous practice showed the phone didn't always pick up as well as she liked.

Placing it on the ledge of the fireplace mantle, which was closer to Henry, might work.

As opposed to acting secretive, she strolled over to the mantle and rearranged the knick-knacks including the phone in the arrangement. *Genius.* She wanted to share her sudden revelation but held her tongue and allowed Henry to answer her question as she returned to her seat.

"He got much, much better. I not only befriended him but coached him. I wanted him to show up the jerks in the club. He was a natural and became so good he routinely won every game. It was more than enough to cause the club members to resent him."

Mark finally chose to speak, lifting one eyebrow as he did so. "Did you resent him?"

"No, not at first. We went to different colleges but stayed in touch. He was busy beating people I didn't know at D and D. There are online groups, too. We both graduated, came back to the same town, and got together with a few other guys for an occasional game. There are even team tournaments, and the biggest are at Gen Con events. We were planning to be a team for this Gen Con."

Okay, this whole thing was moving forward at the pace of the last ice age. She'd like to speed it up. "Did you kill Joseph Carpenter?"

Mark's mouth dropped open, but thankfully, nothing came out, which may have made it hard to hear Henry's soft reply.

"Technically, no. The snake venom killed him. I didn't want him dead, just out of the tournament. Without him, I could be the leader and champion, which I was certain would impress Sasha."

Donna gave the self-confessed murderer the once over. Unfortunately, she'd met more killers than she ever wanted to in her lifetime. Most were only passing through Legacy, and a few had even booked at her inn. Still, this one had to be the most unlikely of all. Sweat popped out on the brow of the trembling man.

Henry MacGyver perched on the edge of the cushy wingchair. His legs were pressed close together and his shoulders slightly pitched as if he'd jump out of the chair or take flight to fly away from his confession.

Mark sucked in his lips, then spoke. "Snake venom?"

"Yes." Henry bobbed his head. "Most people will not die from a snake bite, even if it is poisonous."

"There are definite consequences," Donna hurried to correct him, "such as losing a limb. It depends. The individual's size and pre-existing health conditions also figure into it."

Henry closed his eyes as if shutting out Donna's words. Then, he snapped them open, surprising her. "I discovered that." He choked out the words ending with a sob. "He was only supposed to get sick. I would have rushed him to the hospital where they would have administered the anti-venom. He'd be saved, and I'd go on to captain the winning team since he'd be weak from the experience. Sasha would finally notice me. I wouldn't be just another nerdy guy fixated on her, but he was never a big guy and with his asthma, he never stood a chance."

There were holes in his story. Sure, she believed he was the killer. Why else would he be confessing to a death that everyone had written off as a fatal allergy attack? "What type of snake venom? Where did you get it?"

"I think it was coral snake. All I know for sure is that it was from the Elapidae family. That's what it said on the vial."

While coral snake bites were rare with the snake not wanting to see humans as much as humans didn't want to see it, the effects included respiratory difficulties and shutdown, which would be exacerbated by asthma. "Sounds about right for that type of snake. Still, where do you get that kind of stuff?"

Henry's eyes widened, and he held his hand up in a stop gesture. "I don't want to say anything that will get anyone in trouble, especially since they had no clue I took the venom"

Mark stood and waved his hand in her direction, signaling she should table her comments for a moment. Mark paced slowly around the room with his hands behind his back, appearing to deliberate on the subject at hand as opposed to questioning a murderer, "I know, Henry, that snake venom is available online. It's used for antidotes and aphrodisiacs, although I suspect most of that stuff isn't real. It's expensive, but not real. The power comes from people believing it *is*."

What was her husband doing? Her hospital emergency room had treated more than one man who tried to use the venom as an aphrodisiac. Some mistakenly assumed if a little was good, then a lot would be great. Gossip that salacious naturally spread around the hospital.

"Oh no, it was real. There's some research going on about making an anti-venom pen that hikers can carry with them. My friend, Mike, is working in a lab that is doing it. Anyhow, he asked me to take care of his birds while he was gone on a long weekend." His upheld hand migrated to his throat. "Mike had no clue. He's not to blame."

Donna had serious doubts that the bird-loving Mike had left the venom out in plain sight, available for easy theft. She was sure the lab had an inventory of every vial of venom they bought. It made her wonder why Mike had even brought it home, but she had a suspicion.

"Understandable," Mark agreed as if the whole thing was little more than a prank, "but how did you liberate the snake venom?"

Ah, she saw what he did there. Changed the word *stole* to *liberate* as if the snake venom needed to be freed. How would Henry explain that detail?

"I had a key to his apartment. I went back with a small container and poured some of the venom into it. I added some vegetable oil to take its place in the vial."

Not only had the man murdered and stole, but he would also set back the snake venom antidote pen research. Maybe she should at least give a heads up if she knew what research lab to call. Good chance they might start increasing the potency of the injections on test subjects if they thought the tampered vial was ineffective. She couldn't have that whether the test subjects were four-legged as opposed to two.

Mark spoke in his deep, soothing voice that he used to pull confessions. "You planned a trip back to Mike's apartment to steal the venom?"

"Yes," Henry volunteered the information unaware he'd just confessed to premeditated murder or at the very least, attempted.

The pacing stopped, and Mark assumed his thoughtful pose with one hand behind his back and the other folded across his chest. All he needed was a smoking pipe to complete his literary sleuth look. His brows beetled, and he shook his head. "I'm not sure you're capable of murder. You seem like a nice, young man. I can't imagine you overpowering your friend and injecting him with the venom."

Henry's eyes brightened, possibly imagining he found a way out. "I would never do that! He wasn't supposed to die!" His last word turned into a wail and buried his face in his hands.

Mark gave her the slightest head waggle to let her know it was her turn. Without being told, her role would be the unsympathetic listener or bad cop. It wouldn't be that hard since Henry had admitted to planning out the murder, although he kept saying it wasn't murder as if that negated the fact that Joseph was dead. Personally, she wanted to pry his hands off his face to see if he was really crying. Her bet was he wasn't.

Learning from the best, she slid closer to the chair to use her height to her advantage. She lowered her voice a tad and asked in what she considered her best con man wheedle, "How did you do it?"

His head came up a little exposing his eyes that were just as clear as when he walked in. Yep, just as she thought, no tears.

"I told him we needed to take vitamin B12 shots to have the energy to be sharp through the gaming. Told him all the other gamers were doing it. He wasn't too thrilled about it since he used to take shots for allergies. He used to be super allergic to bees."

Henry delivered the information very matter-of-factly, and her expression must have said as much.

He swayed and muttered, "Joseph, Joseph, whatever will I do without my friend?"

She couldn't be sure, but she was pretty sure he'd be doing between five and ten years or maybe more, depending on the judge. As the bad cop, she needed to slam him down as opposed to giving him a reassuring pat on the back. *Think, Donna.*

"You didn't care about him. It was all about you. You're not fooling anyone. You wanted to be the leader, *The Champ*, the important one if only to impress Sasha." She had a suspicion, but nothing to back it up, but she thought she'd run it by Henry and see if he'd bite. "Joseph had eyes for Sasha, too. You had to make sure he didn't get her, didn't you?" She smacked her fist into her hand to hammer the point home.

Henry jumped up out of his chair, his cheeks flushed and his eyes glassy. "Yes, I wanted to be number one for a change. I taught him all I knew, shielded him from the bullies, and he repaid me by being better than me, attracting all the attention and glory."

Yep, it sounded like a confession to her, although she had to wonder how much glory was involved in a simple board game that went on for hours. Anything recorded without the suspect's permission wasn't admissible in court, but he didn't know that. There was also the fact he chose to tell a Legacy law enforcement officer. It sounded like Henry gave himself up, the question was why?

"Did you disguise yourself as Joseph to register at the inn?"

Henry shook his head. "Just the beanie and glasses. You know. Tennyson told you. For a while I thought I'd gotten away with it, then I saw Ten in town and he gave me a long, knowing look."

Donna could have told him that long look meant nothing. Still, if it made the man think twice about his actions, then it was all good.

Mark held up his hand. "Okay. I can accept you registered as Joseph. What about the body?"

A heavy sigh came from Henry. "I tried to get him to a hospital."

"Not hard enough." Donna felt obliged to point out the obvious. "Even after he died you could have brought him in. He would have been diagnosed as snake bite victim." No reason to point out the single needle mark would not add up to fangs.

His shoulders went up a little as he grimaced, then he shook his head and held his hands out. "I freaked. I drove around for a while trying to find a hospital, but I'm not familiar with the area."

Bad acting, if you asked her. "Heard of GPS? Phone?"

His hands went up to cover his face as he spoke. "I freaked. What part don't you understand about freaked?"

Yeah, she could see a person freaking, but the more he talked the more it appeared premediated. No mention of how the body got upstairs, then she remembered the elevator trials. "Did you stuff Joseph into a cooler and get the elevator guys to send it up?"

He lifted his head and nodded. Well, that answered that. Still there were so many unanswered questions. Mark cleared his throat.

"Walk us through what happened, starting with Joseph's death."

"Okay." He gave a heavy sigh and pushed back into the chair. "Panicked. Drove around wildly looking for a hospital."

Yeah, and she was an appaloosa horse. Donna made a derisive snort.

Mark gave her a look that told her to table her editorial comments. As much as she hated to comply it might help the story unfold faster. Henry kept talking despite her snort.

"When I realized he was dead, I found a desolate stretch of road, dumped our jumbo cooler and put Joseph in it. It was difficult getting it back into the car. He's a little guy, but still heavy."

Donna sucked in her lips saying nothing. Henry gave a short nod in her direction.

"I did convince the elevator men to send up the cooler, which was good since I could never heft it. Later, I brought it down at night."

Mark gestured upward. "I assume you pushed him down the stairs."

"I dragged him mostly, then pushed him down the last bit. I screamed when I reached the foyer, then darted out the side door to my car and left."

Even though everything happened so fast, she could remember a car leaving the parking lot before they darted toward the house. Mark moved his hand slightly, letting Donna know she was back on.

Still retaining her position as bad cop, she queried in a deadpan voice. "Did you get it? The glory? The tournament title? Sasha?"

"No." He abruptly sat and stared off into the distance.

Mark opened up one of the folding chairs she had resting against the wall ready to be carried up to storage and sat. "Would you like to tell me what did happen?"

"Not really." He gave a heavy sigh. "Might as well, though, since it's no secret. I thought I'd naturally be the leader since Joseph made me his co-captain. Turned out that was merely an honorary title. They voted among themselves for Declan to be the group head when Joseph died. Declan didn't even stay. He left our group for the one that placed second. We managed to recruit Sloane so we could participate in the tournament. We placed fourth out of five teams! With our skill levels we should have at least been in the top three. Worse, Sasha bugged out after her character died. Didn't even stay to the end. Giblet told me she'd taken off to some winery with a guy she'd just met. A wine tasting!" He threw up his hands as if he thought a wine tasting was a lame excuse for not sitting through a tournament.

Maybe Sasha got wind that her admirer might not be entirely stable and decided to put some distance between Henry and her. There might not even have been a wine tasting. Even now the much-celebrated Sasha could be home binge-watching something on television. It sounded like a more pleasant prospect than having one more murder attached to the inn.

There was only one more lingering question. "What was with the unicorn mask?"

Surprisingly, Henry laughed. "That was me. You go to any of these conventions and there are always people walking around wearing unicorn masks. Some are unicorn role players, but most do it for a laugh or fun. At one of our meetings, Sasha joked about any guy man enough to wear a unicorn mask had her."

It all made sense now. "Did you think using the mask would prevent the identification of Joseph?"

"Not prevent it, but slow things down enough to allow me time to get away."

The culprit might be wringing his hands and confessing to accidental homicide, but he had to be a cool cucumber to come back to the inn every night and joke with his team members. In the beginning, she thought he was a kid who made a bad decision, but now, she didn't know. Who stuffs their best friend in a cooler? It also pointed out to her that anyone could be a killer with enough motivation.

Chapter Twenty-Two

THE DAY WAS bright and a slight breeze from the ocean made the task a little less somber. Father Ray agreed not only to perform the service but allowed the unknown woman to be buried in the church cemetery. Maria bounced a fussy Cici while Daniel made faces at his daughter trying to entertain her. Cecilia brought flowers that Sloane passed out.

Donna stood clutching the carnation as the slender wooden box was lowered into the ground. Even though Father Ray had given the standard prayer, it didn't feel like enough.

"I hope you're at peace." She dropped the carnation into the grave and onto the box. The others followed suit, each one whispering a wish for the long-ago woman who had such a short life.

Mark took her arm and guided her to the car. "Donna Tollhouse Taber, you have a kind heart."

"No more than you. The difference is everyone knows you do. As for me, it's a secret."

He chuckled and patted her hand. "It's not as big of a secret as you think. I have a way of seeing through you."

The man sounded mighty confident. "Do you know what I have planned for your surprise?"

"A trip to the New York Police Museum?"

She did a double take. "How did you know I looked that up?"

"Computer history."

"That's dirty!" She elbowed him. "It's closed, although a trip to The Big Apple might be fun. No, I decided we could head west, visit the Ozarks, and dig up some diamonds."

"They have diamond mines nearby?"

"Arkansas. Did I surprise you?"

He interlaced his fingers with hers and gave a slight squeeze. "You did. Any reason you picked Arkansas?"

It burned him that he couldn't figure out her plans ahead of time. She was smart enough not to use the home computer or tell anyone. "I've heard it's a quiet place. It would give us a chance to relax. No conventions, skeletons, or suspicious deaths."

"Keep that thought." Mark turned his head toward her so she'd see his wink.

THE END

Donna's Easy Hand-Held Foods for People on the Go

Legacy Lemonade

Ingredients
6 lemons
1 cup of white sugar*
6 cups of cold water

Directions

Juice lemons to equal a cup of juice. (You can also use bottled lemon juice if you're in a hurry)

In a gallon pitcher, combine one cup of lemon juice, sugar, and water. Stir. Chill and serve over ice

*Sugar substitute can be used, but not a cup. Adjust for desired sweetness.

Neighborhood Confab Burger

Cook it on the grill and watch your neighbors show up to *talk*.

Ingredients
1-pound ground lean (7% fat) beef.
1 large egg.
½ cup minced onion.
¼ cup fine dried breadcrumbs.
1 tablespoon Worcestershire.
1 or 2 cloves garlic, peeled and minced.
½ teaspoon salt.
¼ teaspoon pepper

Directions

In a bowl, mix ground beef, egg, onion, breadcrumbs, Worcester-shire, garlic, ½ teaspoon salt, and ¼ teaspoon pepper until well blended. Divide mixture into four equal portions and shape each into a patty about 4 inches wide. (Recipe can be doubled or tripled if needed—it will be needed.)

Cook on oiled grilled to prevent sticking. Serve on buns. Goes well with pickles, lettuce, onions, and tomatoes, too.

Breakfast Sandwiches

There's a Vegetarian in the Inn Sandwich

Ingredients
1 Tbsp olive oil
2 large eggs (Cage-free preferred)
Salt and pepper to taste
Tbsp of butter (softened)
2 slices of Italian bread
1 oz. slice of Swiss cheese
1 oz. slice of cheddar cheese
½ ripe avocado (thinly sliced)

Directions
1. Heat olive oil in a skillet over medium heat. Crack eggs in the pan. Cook and flip until done. Salt and pepper as needed. Transfer to a plate.
2. Butter bread slices.
3. Heat skillet over medium heat. Lay bread butter side down.

Layer Swiss cheese, one fried egg, Cheddar cheese, next fried egg, avocado on top of one bread slice and top with remaining slice. Carefully flip, then cook until bread is heated through and cheese is a little melty. Remove from skillet, cut in half and serve.

Serves: one or two if the person is willing to share.

There's a Big Kid in the Inn Sandwich

Ingredients

2 Tbsp Nutella spread

2 English Muffins

1 sliced banana

2 Tbsp marshmallow cream

Directions

1. Spread Nutella on one half of the English Muffin.
2. Arrange bananas on top of the Nutella topped muffin.
3. Spread marshmallow cream on the other muffin. Press both halves together to make a sandwich.

Serves: one

A Bark in the Night

The Talking Dog Detective Agency
Book One

Chapter One

A GROAN ESCAPED the silent watcher as the girl pulled out a bunch of keys to unlock the front door. The dog that had been sitting now silently stood, his ears alert, his head slowly swinging side to side as he emitted a low growl.

"Damn it." He hadn't counted on a dog. Who takes a dog with them to an office building anyhow? He could have knocked down the girl and grabbed the keys, and finally made it into the building. He'd spent the last six months trying to enter the place.

The few remaining offices weren't open to the public. He'd even donned delivery outfits and tried to get buzzed in. All he managed to discover was no one in the building had water delivered or even a pizza. Usually, he received no reply when he buzzed. It could be that the buzzer didn't work. The building itself was circa 1930s and only the bottom floor was stores, while the rest were apartments or offices.

That would have worked fine if there was an actual store on the first floor instead of empty rooms. He'd considered breaking in, but he'd most likely get caught and end up back in the slammer. Something he'd prefer to avoid since he had more enemies inside than he did out. Now, he'd have to rethink the situation. Once the girl and her dog entered the building, he tucked his hands into his jacket pocket to feel the short length of pipe he'd hidden there. A man had to protect himself, but as a felon, a gun would automatical-

221

ly earn a huge fine and possibly incarceration. Things he wanted to avoid.

Hands still in pockets, he strolled in the direction of Monument Circle. Sweat dotted his face due to the early heat wave. He could have pulled off his sweatshirt, but the hoodie provided conformity that made him almost invisible.

In the center of the city stood a huge war monument reaching toward the heavens as if trying to touch the departed or at least send a message they hadn't been forgotten. He couldn't remember when it had been built—sometime after the Civil War. As a kid, his grandfather had taken him there. With each war, more statues and flat memorials engraved with names appeared. He remembered fingering the names thinking the people only became important by dying. That wasn't going to be him. Nope, he'd had enough of being Toby Nobody. Once he got into the building, he'd find what was his by right and buy that sailboat he fantasized about while doing time. Might even sail around the world.

Foot and vehicle traffic picked up as he made his way to the circle. A horse-driven carriage, complete with picture-snapping tourists, passed him on one side. The harness bells jingled with the horse's movements. He was not sure why a person would even bell a horse. The animal was too large to miss. Then again, maybe the owner thought it made the experience more festive. Toby stopped and watched the slow-moving carriage. He'd never taken a carriage ride, never took a gondola ride down the canal, either. Nope, those things were for tourists or people with a lot of throwaway money. Soon, that would be him, as soon as he got rid of the obstacles.

NALA PLACED ONE hand on her hip and kept a tight grip on the leash clipped to a handsome black German shepherd mix as she surveyed the building. The stone façade building rose a good five stories, nothing compared to the other buildings looming behind it on a more visited street in Indianapolis. The morning sun revealed chipped parts of the façade and the crumbling entrance steps, exposing the underlying concrete block structure.

"The building has character." She glanced up and down the street, noticing the lack of foot traffic during the early day. The ground floor windows revealed empty rooms inside where light spots on the industrial gray carpet revealed where furniture once sat. "I was never shown a ground floor office or even one with wrapa-round windows." Her shoulders went up in a shrug. "It is just as well. Anyone visiting a private eye doesn't want to be on display. I probably couldn't afford it anyhow. Let's go see *our* office."

The dog gave a bark as if he understood. Nala's straight hair swung into her face as she bent to pat the animal. "That's right, Max. It's a new start for both of us."

Max and Nala climbed the first flight of stairs in silence. By the time they reached the second flight, a young man with a dark hipster beard and arms full of labeled boxes met them.

"Hey, a dog, cool!"

A bark greeted his assessment while Nala offered her hand, then pulled it back as she realized he couldn't shake. "Hello. Do you need any help with your boxes?"

"No, I'm good. I'm sure you're not coming to see me. I'd re-member if I had a beautiful woman and her equally handsome dog coming to see me."

A nervous laugh greeted his remark. Blatant flirting rattled Nala since it was difficult to pinpoint if it was sincere. Extroverts could reply with clever comebacks in a second, while people like herself struggled for an appropriate reply long after the person had left. "Yeah, right."

Instead of insisting he meant it, the man grinned. "I'm Harry Chafant. I run a mail-order business on the second floor. Didn't know there were any other businesses in the building. There are some apartments in use, though. Maybe you're here to see one of the residents."

Nala shoved her hands in her jeans pockets since she didn't know what to do with them. "Ah, I'm Nala, Nala Bonne." *Oops*, she had lost a chance to try out her new name. "I'll be opening my business on the third floor. Max," she gestured to her dog, "and I are going up to check out the office."

"Really?" Harry drew out the word, and his smile grew bigger. "Today must be my lucky day. I'm headed to the post office, but when I get back I'd love to show you around."

"Thanks, but I've already seen the building." Regret stabbed her as she watched the man's smile slip. No good would come out of being too friendly to her neighbors. Even if they did hit it off, eventually they'd break up and she'd peer out her door every time a woman got buzzed in, wondering if it was her replacement. Still, she didn't want to sound unfriendly. She held up one hand. "See ya around."

"Yeah," Harry agreed and continued to descend the stairs.

If her best friend, Karly, had witnessed the scene, she'd take Nala to task, telling her she shot down another perfectly good prospect. Maybe she had, but she also avoided a messy emotional entanglement and the possibility of placing another crack in her heart. Some women threw themselves into the dating game with all the intensity of a bullfighter. A failed romance never seemed to get them down. They would just move on to the next guy. The most amazing thing about it was that there was always a next guy. In her experience, most men never passed her father's background investigation test. Oh, the joys of having a father in law enforcement.

On the third-floor landing, Nala withdrew her key to the office and opened the door. The entry office remained dusty and empty. The furniture fairies hadn't appeared overnight, not that she'd expected them to. A few words to her mother would have her scouring the design warehouse for office furniture, but she wouldn't mention it. This was something Nala wanted to accomplish on her own. With helpful, somewhat overprotective parents she seldom felt like she did much on her own. Even with school projects, she had felt they were more a group project.

Her father had built a circuit board that allowed an electrical circuit to run several items at once for the science fair. She, however, had wanted to grow plants and play music to them. When she didn't ace the science fair, her father demanded to know if the fair was fixed. It was obvious the circuit board was the superior project. Her petite teacher went toe to toe with her father and pointed out the circuit board was beyond the ability of a seven-year-old. A third-grader won with an experiment that showed tomato plants grew taller with regular shots of diet cola.

"Let's hit it." Nala dropped the leash and allowed Max to wander at will while she withdrew window cleaner, a rag, and some press-on letters. Her first project would be the exterior door.

"I'm not sure about the clear glass. If a person wants privacy they don't want everyone and their cousin peering in at them as they come to me to consult about a philandering husband or wife."

"Do people even do that anymore? I just thought they divorced, divvied up the stuff, and sometimes offloaded the family pet to a friend, relative, or took him for a ride in the country."

Nala blinked, knowing good and well no one else was in the office. She dropped her gaze to Max, who had his head cocked as if waiting for her answer. *No, it couldn't be.* Dogs didn't talk, at least not in a raspy baritone. She pinched herself just to be certain she wasn't dreaming. It hurt. *Maybe she just thought he said something. The best thing would be to test out her theory.* "Did your last owners divorce?"

Something must have happened to Max since she had picked him up at an animal shelter the day before he would have been put down. Grown dogs were only kept for a few days at the most. Then again, it could be she wanted Max to talk so she'd have someone to converse with. A fellow traveler in this new life she'd plotted out for herself.

"Nope." He grimaced, showing his teeth. "I made the mistake of talking again. Not the first time I've been ousted from a comfortable home. This last time I was driven from the house by my former owner holding a crucifix and calling me *devil dog.*"

"Weird." She shook her head hard still not convinced she wasn't dreaming. I would have thought someone would have put you on the David Letterman show. Whoops, I keep forgetting he retired." *Was she really having a conversation with her dog?*

"You'd think that." He barked a couple of times before continuing. "You gotta remember English is my third language and some things don't translate."

"You speak three languages?"

He lifted his nose with pride. "I do. Dog, of course, the silent language of scent, and I'm reasonably conversant in English. One potential owner tried to speak to me in German. Despite my muddied bloodlines, I couldn't understand a word he said. I wanted to tell him I was born in America. I didn't, since I wasn't totally sure." .

"Ah, of course." She nodded her head as if she understood. *Was there anything understandable about a talking dog?* "So, when did you start talking? Are there a lot of talking dogs out there?"

His nose dropped as he stretched out and laid his head on his paws. "All dogs talk in the accepted canine dialect, except for basenjis who do this strange yodeling thing. I haven't met one who speaks English, although most do understand it very well. They might pretend not to know phrases such as stay off the couch, not for you, or not now. They do. Even though they understand English, they freak out when I say something. Something about it being us against them, meaning your kind."

"Ah." Nala searched her mind for how she had treated Max in the few days she owned him. Had she offended him somehow by treating him like a dog? "You never answered how you came to talk."

"Oh, that." He managed a few sharp yips that resembled a laugh. "Funny story. My first owner was a close-mouthed male. Not one to share his feelings or general observations about life. While this didn't bother me all that much, it was an entirely different story for his girlfriend, who happened to be a witch. She always fixed extra scrambled eggs and bacon for me when she visited, so I liked her. Anyhow, one day, she says to the man, 'If you don't talk to me, then your dog will.'"

"Just like that?"

"Took me a while to become a good conversationalist. At the time, I was so excited I voiced every thought." He lifted his head enough to display a doggy grin. "Imagine a constant litany of me listing everything I saw. Tree, grass, dog poop from the poodle two houses down, smells like she likes me. After all, she left it in front of my house. Well, you get the idea."

"Irritating."

"Yep, I discovered immediately that while people yack non-stop, they don't appreciate a talkative dog, especially my first owner who didn't even make the effort to talk to his girlfriend. One day, she was gone. Not sure if they agreed to separate. I just noticed the house smelled less like the sandalwood incense she always burned. After that, I got relocated, too."

"Where?"

"A family with kids. They had a little boy I adored. He wasn't that good at walking so he often hung onto me when he was unstable. It was only natural that I tried to encourage him. His parents were worried about his developing psyche and the dangers of believing a dog could talk. They thought I was a bad influence." Max stood, paced to the hallway and returned to his original place before circling and flopping back down on the floor.

"That's too bad about the kid. I'm not sure what I'll do with a talking dog."

A foul smell permeated the air. "Sorry." Max offered her an apologetic expression. "The Chinese food you gave me yesterday doesn't agree with me. I love it, though. Besides, stress has that effect, too."

Her intention had been to get a dog for companionship. Karly, who worked at the shelter, had emailed her pictures of dogs that would be put down. *Talk about guilt.* Even worse, when they met for lunch, she'd talk about the abandoned dogs, giving them names and listing their idiosyncrasies. Nala pointed out more than once that if Karly wanted someone to adopt a dog it was better not to mention things such as its tendency to rip up anything vaguely chewable or its midnight howling. Karly insisted people had to enter relationships with open eyes.

As if that would ever work. Women shoved themselves into shapewear, piled on the makeup, and clipped on hair extensions under the belief that men didn't want reality. She was sure women didn't either. On occasion, when they needed a reality check, they'd hire an investigator. She'd specialize in date research. No woman wanted to go on a date with an online prospect or even the cousin of a co-worker and end up battered, broke or, worse, dead.

"We'll have to limit your intake to the weekends. Can't have you scaring off the clients with your toxic farts."

A hopeful gleam appeared in Max's eyes as his ears pitched forward. "Do you mean you're going to keep me?"

"Why not?"

"The talking usually scares people off, but Karly assured me you'd be okay with it. Since you're into magic, psychic skills, and all that." His long tail wagged, hitting the floor. The empty room magnified the sound.

"Karly knew? The woman who never believes in too much information withheld the fact from me that you could speak?"

"She never told you she didn't like Jeff, either."

Nala looked up from pecking at her cell with her index finger. "You mean you and Karly talked about my ex-boyfriend?"

Max swallowed hard. "You know, I could be an immense help around the detective agency."

"How so?"

"Scent. I can tell if people are lying or not by their scent."

She shook her head, imagining how well a large German shepherd mix sniffing them would go over. "I'm pretty sure my future clients and suspects wouldn't go for you sticking your nose in their crotch."

"Please." He managed a huff. "I have excellent scent ability. The nose in the crotch thing is something dogs do just for fun. It's a game we like to play with humans. If you didn't react so strongly, then it wouldn't be as hilarious."

Author Notes

If you enjoyed this book, try checking out the entire series. Available at all online retailers.

The first four books are available in Large Print and Audio.

Murder Mansion

Drop Dead Handsome

Killer Review

Christmas Calamity

Death Pledges a Sorority

Caribbean Catastrophe

Weddings Can Be Murder

The Skeleton Wore Diamonds

- ➤ The best way to encourage an author is to write a review.
- ➤ Do you have an idea for a story, recipe or a character name? Love to hear it. I can be reached through my website www.morgankwyatt.com.
- ➤ *One lucky reader had a character named after her in this book. Find out how you can be in a book by becoming a newsletter subscriber.*
- ➤ Want to get free books, read excerpts before everyone else, receive special members only swag and giveaways? You need to be on the newsletter mailing list. Go over to my website and sign up.
- ➤ Do you like humor with your suspense? Check out the new cozy mystery series, *The Talking Dog Detective Agency.*
- ➤ Love to meet you, check out my personal appearances on the website too.
- ➤ Can you do one more thing? Read. It's good for you!

M. K. Scott

www.ingramcontent.com/pod-product-compliance
Lightning Source LLC
Chambersburg PA
CBHW060428180626
46817CB00007B/2722